THE GEMINI RISING ROCKIN' MACHINE

THE GEMINI ANGELIC DEMON DANCE

The Gemini Angelic Demon Dance
Featuring Books
Book Thirteen: Gemini Dance
Book Fourteen: Gemini Beast
Featuring The Story
Hell Night At Demon House

Copyright 2016 by The Gemini Rising Rockin' Machine

**ISBN-13: 978-0692789407 (Gemini Rising Rockin'
Machine,The)**
ISBN-10: 0692789405

For questions, comments you may send correspondence to.

thegeminirisingrockinmachine@twc.com

Official Website
www.thegeminirisingrockinmachine.com

The Gemini Angelic Demon Dance (951.)

Ancient-Times of Long-Ago
Tells-The-Tale of Beauty and Ecstasy
That-Can-Become – Mayhem and Murder
At-The-Moment of Climax

Be-Pure – Be-Loving – You-May-Live
Let-Primal-Take-Over – Your-Ecstasy
Watch a Being so Pure and Loving
That-Belongs – In-Heaven

Split-Into a Evil-Beautiful-Being
That-Will-Eat – Your-Flesh
While-Turning – Your-Bones to Dust
Just to Get to Your-Soul

Her-Beauty – Is-Sexy-Death
To-Fallen-Heroes and Fools
Who-Ask-Her – For-Her-Love
When-All-They-Want – Is-Her-Body

(Pre-Chorus)
One Is So Sweet And Pretty
One Is So Evil And Pretty
Dance Baby Dance – Dance Yourself Away
One Will Let You – Have Her Love
One Will Let You – Have Her Hate
Dance Baby Dance – Dance Yourself Away

(Chorus)
The Gemini Angelic Demon Dance
Is A Blast – When It's Full Of Love
The Gemini Angelic Demon Dance
Turns Into Hell – When It's Full Of Lust
The Gemini Angelic Demon Dance
Enjoy Free True Love And Live
The Gemini Angelic Demon Dance
Enjoy Taking In The Lust And Die Fast

She-Lives-Forever – She-Never-Dies
Dawn of Each-Century – She-Changes
Before-Her-Curse – She-Was-Mortal
Her-Beauty – Enraged-The-Queen

2

Under-The-Moon – The-Witch's-Spell
Inserted-Evil – Inside-Her-Soul
Turning-This-Sweet – Lovely-Lady-Into
The-Gemini-Angelic-Demon

Her-Lover – Wanted-Love
She-Gave-Him – Her-Love
Just-Like-Before – First-Came-Passion
The-Moments – Before-Climax
Her-Lover's-Love – Turned-Into-Lust

The-Greed of Her-Lover
Turned-Her-Blood – Ice-Cold
Flames-From-Hell – Boiled-Her-Soul
She-Watched in Horror as The-Demon-Inside-Her
Killed-Her-Lover and Ate-His-Soul

The- Demon – Back-Inside-Her
Screaming – With-Blood on Her-Hands
She-Ran and She-Ran – Praying to God

Her-Heart-Pounding – Out of Her-Chest
She-Stopped-Running – Hearing a Voice
Inside-Her-Mind – That-Froze-Her-Solid
Telling-Her to Find – Another-Man to Lust
So-The-Gemini-Angelic-Demon-Dance – Continues-On

(Pre-Chorus)
One Is So Sweet And Pretty
One Is So Evil And Pretty
Dance Baby Dance – Dance Yourself Away
One Will Let You – Have Her Love
One Will Let You – Have Her Hate
Dance Baby Dance – Dance Yourself Away

(Chorus)
The Gemini Angelic Demon Dance
Is A Blast – When It's Full Of Love
The Gemini Angelic Demon Dance
Turns Into Hell – When It's Full Of Lust
The Gemini Angelic Demon Dance
Enjoy Free True Love And Live
The Gemini Angelic Demon Dance
Enjoy Taking In The Lust And Die Fast

3

(The Demon Inside Speaks)
You're-Heaven, I'm-Hell – You're-Love, I'm-Hate
You're-Cursed – You-Will-Never-Die
You-Have-No-Choice – You-Have-No-Will
You're-Cursed – You-Will-Live-Forever

Men-Will-Ask-You to Enjoy-Your-Body
You-Will-Say-Yes – You-Will-Never-Say-No
If-Loves is Inside – One of Their-Hearts
They-Will-Live and Your-Curse-Will-End
If-Lust is Inside – Their-Heart
I-Will-Feast on Their-Soul
As-The-Dance – Continues-On and On
(The Demon Inside Stops Speaking)

Ancient-Times of Long-Ago – Tells-The-Tale of Beauty and Ecstasy
That-Can-Become – Mayhem and Murder at The-Moment of Climax
Her-Beauty is Sexy-Death to Fallen-Heroes and Fools
Who-Ask-Her for Her-Love – When-All-They-Want is Her-Body

She-Lives-Forever-She-Never-Dies – Dawn of Each-Century
She-Changes – Before-Her-Curse – She-Was-Mortal
Her-Beauty – Enraged-The-Queen – For-The-Queen-Was-Ugly
Under-The-Moon – The-Witch's-Spell – Inserted-Evil-Inside-Her-Soul
Turning-This-Sweet – Lovely-Lady-Into
The-Gemini-Angelic-Demon

(Pre-Chorus)
One Is So Sweet And Pretty
One Is So Evil And Pretty
Dance Baby Dance – Dance Yourself Away
One Will Let You – Have Her Love
One Will Let You – Have Her Hate
Dance Baby Dance – Dance Yourself Away

(Chorus)
The Gemini Angelic Demon Dance
Is A Blast – When It's Full Of Love
The Gemini Angelic Demon Dance
Turns Into Hell – When It's Full Of Lust
The Gemini Angelic Demon Dance
Enjoy Free True Love And Live
The Gemini Angelic Demon Dance
Enjoy Taking In The Lust And Die Fast

Book Thirteen: Gemini Dance (Pages 5-38)

(Side One)
241. Gemini Dance (09.)
242. My Sweet Dead Lady (14.)
243. Dancing With Evil (631.)
244. Hot Evil Halloween Lady (632.)
    Kiss Of Death (Take Two) **(910.)**
245. Pretty Naked Dancing Evil Lady (636.)

(Side Two)
(From Horny Sinner To Hell Flunky: 246-250)
246. Repent You Horny Sinner (626.)
247. You're The Whore Of Babylon (627.)
248. Help Me (Save Me Satan) (628.)
249. In Life He Had No One (629.)
250. Hell Flunky (630.)

(Side Three)
251. I'm Sorry Lady (You're Dead Already) (364.)
252. You're Dead (I Can't Love You) (468.)
253. She's Not Dead (220.)
254. Evil Love (700.)
    Teach Me How To Growl **(829.)**
255. Satanic Lady Of The Night (740.)
    Rock And Roll Demon Man **(907.)**

(Side Four)
(Vampire Friends: 256-257)
256. Lick The Blood Off Your Fingers (819.)
257. Belly Full Of Blood (820.)
(Thirteen Witches With Thirteen Evil Sons: 258-260)
258. Thirteen Witches (633.)
259. Thirteen Evil Sons In Two Parts: (634.)
    I. The Spell Of Protection
    II. Die This Darkened Night
260. The Curse / The Rise Of The 13ᵗʰ Witch (635.)

(Bonus Songs)
Evil Lady (425.)
Hello Lady Of Death (553.)

241. Gemini Dance

Party – Sex – Burn
The – Gemini – Dance
Dance – Baby – Dance
The – Gemini – Dance
Dance – Yourself – Away!

We-Are-Dancing – Chanting-Around-The-Fire
The-Air-Is so Magical-This-Night – We-Six-Times-Two
Of- Equal-Amount – Are-Prepared to Be-Enchanted
By-The-Darkness – That-Is-Brought to Life

It's-Time to Drink – Electric-Wine
Gorge-Ourselves – With-Each-Others-Flesh
Splash-Our-Blood – Into-The-Flames
Laughing-In-Delight – Turned-On
At-The-Coming of The-Twin-Demons

(Chorus)
The Gemini Dance Is Fun For All
So Come And Dance If You Dare
But Don't Come Back Bitching
When You Begin To Sizzle From Your
Rendition Of The Gemini Dance

Party – Sex – Burn
The – Gemini – Dance
Dance – Baby – Dance
The – Gemini – Dance
Dance – Yourself – Away!

They-Are a We – That is-Named – Gemini
One-Male – One-Female – That-Counts as One
Split-In-Two – Both so Prefect
We-Six-Men – Enjoy-Her – Sexual-Beauty
We-Six-Women – Enjoy-His – Sexual-Handsomeness

(Chorus)
The Gemini Dance Is Fun For All
So Come And Dance If You Dare
But Don't Come Back Bitching
When You Begin To Sizzle From Your
Rendition Of The Gemini Dance

Party – Sex – Burn
The – Gemini – Dance
Dance – Baby – Dance
The – Gemini – Dance
Dance – Yourself – Away!

Partying and Having-Sexual-Fun
Turns to Pain and Slaughter
Big-Mistake – We-Twelve
Lying on The-Ground – Motionless
For-We-Are – All-Dead

Soon as Gemini – Had-Their-Final-Pleasure
They-Give-Us-Twelve – Our-Final-Kiss
The-Pain-From-This-Kiss – Ripped-Out
Our-Souls – Souls-That-Are-Brought
To-Hell by Gemini to Burn-Forevermore

(Chorus)
The Gemini Dance Is Fun For All
So Come And Dance If You Dare
But Don't Come Back Bitching
When You Begin To Sizzle From Your
Rendition Of The Gemini Dance

Party – Sex – Burn
The – Gemini – Dance
Dance – Baby – Dance
The – Gemini – Dance
Dance – Yourself – Away!

The-Gemini-Dance – Will-Give-You-Pleasure
More-Than-You-Ever – Thought-Possible
If-Asked – While-You're-In-Ecstasy
You-Will-Scream – Oh-Yes!
If-Asked-After – While-You're-Burning
You-Will-Scream – Hell-No!

(Chorus)
The Gemini Dance Is Fun For All
So Come And Dance If You Dare
But Don't Come Back Bitching
When You Begin To Sizzle From Your
Rendition Of The Gemini Dance

242. My Sweet Dead Lady

My-Sweet-Dead-Lady – I-Love-You so Much
I've-Never-Loved – Anyone-Like-You-Before
The-Sweet – Cold-Crisp-Feel of Your-Flesh
I'm so Happy – Come-Dance-With-Me

When-I'm-Sad and Blue
You-Always – Pull-Me-Through
Make-Me-Remember – That-I
Have-You to Love – 'Til-I-Die

(Chorus)
My Sweet Dead Lady
We Fit Together So Right
When My Time Is Up
I Want To Be Laid Next To You
My Sweet Dead Lady
I'm Looking So Forward To
Rotting With You Forever

My-Sweet-Dead-Lady – I-Love-You so Much
Let's-Laugh and Sing – Dance the Night-Away
No-Shame if They – Don't-Understand
Forget the World – We-Know-What – We-Want

We-Know – We're-Different
That-Won't-Stop or Change-Us
'Cause-Our-Love is Strong and True
I-Can't-Wait to Be as Blue as You

(Chorus)
My Sweet Dead Lady
We Fit Together So Right
When My Time Is Up
I Want To Be Laid Next To You
My Sweet Dead Lady
I'm Looking So Forward To
Rotting With You Forever

243. Dancing With Evil

You-Can't-Walk on Water
You-Can't-Fly in The-Sky
But-You – Can-Bleed
You-Can-Die – Why
You-Are-Mortal
Born of This-Earth

Every-Day-Coming-Closer to The-Day
You-Lie-Crying on The-Ground
Mortality – Effecting-Your-Mind
You-No-Longer – Can-Laugh
Love is Lost – Inside-Your-Heart
You've-Become – Afraid of Dying

(Chorus)
My Friend – I'm Here
Reach Out To Me
Your Twisted And Tormented
Soul Of Wanting Despair
Come Dance – Come
Dancing With Evil

Light-The-Candle – Alone in The-Dark
Tears in Your-Eyes – Blood-Dripping
You're-Ready to Lose-Control
Letting-Your-Soul – Fall

Out of Silence – Your-Name is Called
Body and Blood – Frozen-Stiff
Say-Nothing – Stay-Still
Evil-Will-Drift – Back to Hell
Speak-Out – Stand-Up
Evil-Will-Become – Your-Dancing-Partner

(Chorus)
My Friend – I'm Here
Reach Out To Me
Your Twisted And Tormented
Soul Of Wanting Despair
Come Dance – Come
Dancing With Evil

244. Hot Evil Halloween Lady

She's so Fine – She's so Evil
Dream-Ladies be Gone
You're-Too-Sweet – Since-I've
Tasted and Felt – Pure-Evil-Delight

Shake-Your – Evil-Body
Scream – Rip-Out-Your-Hair
Keep the Blood on Your-Hands
When-You-Come – Dancing to Me

(Chorus)
Hot Evil Halloween Lady
Tonight Is Your Night
To Come Back To Life
Hot Evil Halloween Lady
Let Me Be The One To Sex You
In Between All Your – Halloween Slaughter

Midnight-Hour – She-Screams at The-Moon
Her-Eyes – Are-Dark as Coal
While-She's-Evilly – Purring in My-Arms
Biting-My-Neck – Tasting-My-Blood

Dancing-With – No-Love in Her-Soul
She-Takes-Her-Claws – Plunging-Them-Deep
Into-My-Chest – Ripping-Out-My-Heart
Laughs and Giggles – She-Feasts-Fast
On-My-Bleeding-Heart – Before it Gets-Cold

(Chorus)
Hot Evil Halloween Lady
Tonight Is Your Night
To Come Back To Life
Hot Evil Halloween Lady
Let Me Be The One To Sex You
In Between All Your – Halloween Slaughter

She's so Fine – She's so Evil
She-Kissed-Me – She-Bit-Me
She-Killed-Me – She-Ate-My-Heart
She-Has a Fine – Evil-Body
I-Still-Crave – From-My-Grave

Kiss Of Death (Take Two)

Wolf-Howls – Owl-Whoos
As the Snake – Slithers-On the Ground
While-The-Rabbit is Frozen-In-Fear
As a Toad – Hops-By – Unnoticed by All
Except by Her – The-Lady of Death

Moonlight – Shines-Down on Her
Making-Her – Pale-Skin – Glow in Response
Everything is Okay – Everything is Alright
Until-I – Walk-Up to Her – While-She's-Feeding

(Chorus)
Kiss Of Death
One Kiss Is All I Get
Kiss Of Death
Twice Would Be So Nice
Kiss Of Death
No-Sex-After – Just-Death
And A Whole Lot Of Hell

Beautiful – She-Is
This-Lady of Death
I-Cannot-Move – I-Cannot-Talk
As-This-Lady of Death
Gives-Me-Her – Kiss of Death

Take-Me-Home – Take-Me to Hell
I'm a Sinner – That's-Where-I-Belong
I-Don't-Mind – Just-Please
Lady of Death – One-More-Kiss
Before-I-Burn – Forevermore

(Chorus)
Kiss Of Death
One Kiss Is All I Get
Kiss Of Death
Twice Would Be So Nice
Kiss Of Death
No-Sex-After – Just-Death
And A Whole Lot Of Hell

245. Pretty Naked Dancing Evil Lady

The-Air is Cold
The-Night is Dark
In-Our-Sleepy – Out of Sight
Old-Town – That-Has-Known
Its-Share of Evil

It's-In-The-Air – We-Breathe
It's-Saturated – In-Our-Water
It's-Soaked – Deep-Down
This-Evil – Has-Been-Around
Before-Our-Town – Was-Built

(Chorus)
Dance Your Evil Spells In The Night
Pretty Naked Dancing Evil Lady
Make Us Pay Every Full Moon Night
For Destroying Your Beautiful Forest
So We Could Build Our Homes

We-Broke-Ground
Ready to Carve-Out a Town
For-All-Those – That-Came
Together – On-Our-Journey

Out of The-Beautiful – Green-Forest
Came-Dancing – Out of Nowhere
This-Pretty-Naked – Dancing-Evil-Lady

Chanting and Shaking – Her-Naked
Evil-Body-Around – Making-All-Us-Men
Forget-Our-Wives and Families
Walking-Up to Her – Like-She's
Our-Piper – We-Her-Rats

(Chorus)
Dance Your Evil Spells In The Night
Pretty Naked Dancing Evil Lady
Make Us Pay Every Full Moon Night
For Destroying Your Beautiful Forest
So We Could Build Our Homes

Half the Men – Dead
From an Evil – Spell
The-Other-Half – Not-Caring
Only-Wanting-More – Love-From-The
Pretty-Naked – Dancing-Evil-Lady
Who-Hissed at The-Women
For-Them to Come to Her

Out-In – The-Full-Moon
She-Made – Our-Women-Do-Things
Like-They – Never-Have-Done
To-Themselves-Before
While-We – Men-Watched
Not-Saying a Word

(Chorus)
Dance Your Evil Spells In The Night
Pretty Naked Dancing Evil Lady
Make Us Pay Every Full Moon Night
For Destroying Your Beautiful Forest
So We Could Build Our Homes

The-Whole-Town is Completely
Under-The-Spell of The-Pretty
Naked – Dancing-Evil-Lady
We're-Her-Pets – Every-Full-Moon-Night
Build-Her a Fire – Make-Her a Feast

While-She-Plays – With-Us-Like-Toys
Until-She-Picks – Out-The-Ones
She-Wants to Kill-That-Night
For-Our-Crimes – Against-Her
And-Her-Evil – Hell-Laced-Forest

(Chorus)
Dance Your Evil Spells In The Night
Pretty Naked Dancing Evil Lady
Make Us Pay Every Full Moon Night
For Destroying Your Beautiful Forest
So We Could Build Our Homes

246. Repent You Horny Sinner

Caught-With-His – Hand-Down-His-Pants
Watching the Hot – Lady-Next-Door
Sunbathing in Something – Not-Very-Much
His-God-Loving-Mother – Walked-In on Cue

Screams-Turned to Smacks – With-Cursing
The-Young-Man – With-Natural-Thoughts
Beaten-Down-Once-Again by His
Holy-Mother – The-Hand of God
It's-His-Fault – That-His-Father – Left-Her

(Chorus)
Repent You Horny Sinner
You Should Be Ashamed
God Is Watching You
Repent You Horny Sinner
Remove Your Hand
So I Can Punish – Your Devil-Hood

You're-The-Devil's-Son – Horny-Sinner
God-Does-Not – Love-You – God-Tells-Me-This
Horny-Sinner – Kneel-Down and Pray
Pray for Forgiveness – Pray for Your-Damned-Soul
What-Were-You – Looking at Horny-Sinner
I-See-No-Filth – But-You – Your-Window

In-God's-Name as I-Live and Breathe
The-Whore of Babylon – Next-Door to Me
Horny-Sinner – You're Going to Hell
Now-I-Must-Rid – Earth of This-Whore
Remind-Me to Beat – More of The-Devil
Out of You – When-I-Get-Back

(Chorus)
Repent You Horny Sinner
You Should Be Ashamed
God Is Watching You
Repent You Horny Sinner
Remove Your Hand
So I Can Punish – Your Devil-Hood
14

247. You're The Whore Of Babylon

Divorced and Lonely – Lilith
Has-Worked so Hard – Losing-Weight
Since-Her-Husband – Went-Away
Tonight is Her-Night a Man-Wants-Her
It's-Been so Long – Since-She's-Been-Touched

Out in The-Sun – In-Her-Own-Yard – Sunbathing
Singing-Along-To a Song – Playing on The-Radio
When-God-Lady – From-Next-Door – Comes
Crashing-In on Her – Filled-With-Rage and Hate
Screaming-Out-Loud – For-All to Hear

(Chorus)
You're The Whore Of Babylon
You Tempted My Son
With Your Evil Naked Body
For This You Must Pay – I Will
Send You Back To Hell – Where You Belong

So-Quick – The-Hand of God
Picks-Up a Brick and Smashes-It
Across-Lilith's-Head and Then
One – Two – Ten-Times-More

Lilith is Now-Dead
Not-Hearing the Praying
Going on Above – Her-Dead-Body
From the Crazy – God-Lady – From-Next-Door

(Chorus)
You're The Whore Of Babylon
You Tempted My Son
With Your Evil Naked Body
For This You Must Pay – I Will
Send You Back To Hell – Where You Belong

15

248. Help Me (Save Me Satan)

The-Young-Man – Looks-Out-His-Window
Watching-With a Smile on His-Face
His-Hateful-Mother – Being-Taken-Away
By the Police for Murdering
The-Sexy-Lady – From-Next-Door

Hours of Questions-Later
The-Young-Man is All by Himself
For the First-Time – Master of His-Own-Fate
He-Loves-This-Power – But-Deep-Down
He's-Still – The-Scared-Young-Man
Without-Anyone to Talk to

(Chorus)
Help Me – Save Me Satan
Take Away My Pain
Let Me Serve You
Help Me – Save Me Satan
Give Me The Power To Make
This World Pay For My Birth

One-Hour-Goes-By – Nothing's-Happening
With-The-Stench of Sulfur and The-Heat-From-Hell
Satan-Appears – With-Contract in His-Fiery-Hand

Sign-Here – My-Young-Man – For-Your-New-Power
Very-Good – Very-Good – You're-Such a Fool
You-Did-Not-Ask – For-Any-Protection
Your-Life – Is in My-Hands – I-Say to You
Welcome to Death – I-Hope-You-Enjoy
Burning in Hell – Forevermore

(Chorus)
Help Me – Save Me Satan
Take Away My Pain
Let Me Serve You
Help Me – Save Me Satan
Give Me The Power To Make
This World Pay For My Birth

249. In Life He Had No One

In-Life – He-Had-No-One
Father – Nowhere to Be-Found
Mother-Crazy – From-Heaven and Hell
School-Was a Nightmare – Come-Alive

He-Tried to Push and Fight-Back
Being-Filled-With – Nothing but Doubt
Brought-Himself – Only-More-Pain
Beaten-Down in Front of Everyone

In-Life – He-Had-No-One
No-Friends to Relate-With
No-Girl-Friend to Find-Love-With

Alone-With-His – Very-Alone-Mind
He-Tried to Talk to The-Kids in School
Practicing in The-Mirror
All-He-Got – Was-Looks of Go-Away or
Ridiculed so Intensely – He-Walked-Away

In-Life – He-Had-No-One
He-Tried to Pray to God
But-Felt-Like a Fool – Betrayed-After
Years and Years of No-Answer
Made-Him-Realize – God-Did-Not-Love-Him

He-Tried-One-More – Night of Hard-Praying
The-Next-Night – He-Prayed to Satan
No-Answer-Once-Again – But-He-Felt-Better
Every-Night-After-That – He-Prayed
With-All-His-Heart and Soul to Satan

Then-One-Night – He-Received-His-Answer
A-Command if He-Followed
Would-Change – His-Life-Forever
All-He-Had to Do – Was-Sit in Front of
His-Window-Tomorrow – Touching-Himself

17

250. Hell Flunky

Welcome to Hell – Hell-Flunky
Go-Stand-Over-There and Shut-up
If-You-Speak – Unless-Spoken To
I'll-Beat-You-Down and Step on Your-Face

Is-That-Tears – I-See-In-Your-Eyes
Are-You – Going to Cry
Come-Over-Here – I'll-Give-You
Something to Cry-About – Hell-Flunky

(Chorus)
I Wasted My Life
I Should Have Just Taken Off
Leaving Behind – My Crazy Life
Now I'm Dead – Living In Hell
As Just Another – Hell Flunky

Everyday – I-Wake-Up in Hell
Get-Dressed – Eat-My-Breakfast
Walk-Out-My-Door to My-Job
As-One of Hell's-Janitors

Everyday – Other-Hell-Flunkies
Beat-The-Hell – Out of Me
Stick-My-Face in Piss and Crap
Laughing – Having a Great-Time
All at My – Damned-Expense

(Chorus)
I Wasted My Life
I Should Have Just Took Off
Leaving Behind – My Crazy Life
Now I'm Dead – Living In Hell
As Just Another – Hell Flunky

Every-Night – I-Go-Home
Take a Bath – Eat – Drink-Some Hell-Beer
Crying-Myself to Sleep – Never-Praying

(Repeat Chorus)

18

251. I'm Sorry Lady (You're Dead Already)

Lonely – Dead-Lady
Dressed-All-In-Pink
Walking-Around so Sad – All-Alone
Watching-All the Alive-People
Living-Their – Living-Lives

Worrying-About –Families and Bills
Going-Out to Dinner and Dates
Falling in Love – On a Moonlit-Night
While-All-She-Can-Do is Roam
Wishing-She-Had – One-More-Day

(Chorus)
I'm Sorry Lady
You're Dead Already
If You Want To Tell Me
What You Need Done For You
Maybe I Can Help You Out

Scared-New – Dead-Lady
Dressed-All-In-Blue
Walking-Around – In a Panic
Trying to Get-Anyone to Talk to Her
Freaking-Out as They – Pass-Through-Her

Waiting – Watching-Her-From a Distance
Letting-Her – Passed on Mind
Wrap-Itself-Around to What's-Happening
Hard to Watch – She's-In-Such-Pain
Experience – Knowing it's Best to Wait

(Chorus)
I'm Sorry Lady
You're Dead Already
If You Want To Tell Me
What You Need Done For You
Maybe I Can Help You Out

Dangerous-Mad – Dead-Lady
Dressed-All-In-Black
Learned to Use – Her-Death
As a Hurting-Tool – Against the Living

She-Won't-Listen to Me as I-Try
Telling-Her – That-I'm-There for Her
She-Has so Much – Hate-Inside-Her
For-What – Was-Done to Her

All-For a Person – That's-Been
Dead and Gone – For a Very-Long-Time
I-Can-Tell-This – For-Sure by The-Way
She is Dressed in Yesterday's-Clothes

(Chorus)
I'm Sorry Lady
You're Dead Already
If You Want To Tell Me
What You Need Done For You
Maybe I Can Help You Out

252. You're Dead (I Can't Love You)

In-My-Life – I've-Met and Mated
With a Whole-Lot of Different-Ladies
I've-Had-My-Troubles
Plenty of Sorrows – but
Life-Goes-On so Does-Dating

One-Day as I-Was – Enjoying-Myself
Getting to Know –Someone
Pretty-Soft – Warm and New
Out of The-Corner of Your
Dead-Eyes – You-See-Me

Looking-Like – You-Came-From
Straight-Out of Hell – You-Walked-Up to Us
Ate-My-Date – Licked-Your-Lips
Like a Smart-Man – I-Took the Hell-Off
Saying-Dead-Lady – You're-Not-Eating-Me

20

(Chorus)
You Come From A Nightmare
Stinking To Low Hell
Saying To Me – I Love You
Telling Me You're My One
In Deep Shock I Reply
You're Dead – I Can't Love You

With-Pieces of My-Date
Stuck in Between – Your-Teeth
You-Chase – After-Me-Pleading
That-You-Want – My-Loving
That-You'll be My-Loving
Beautiful – Dead – Lady

For a Dead-Woman – You-Sure-Are
Fast on Your – Dead-Feet
Noticing-This as I-Run-Faster
While-You – Shorten-Your-Distance

Picking-Up – My-Speed
Turning-Fast – Around a Corner
You-Come – Around-Faster
Wanting-Me – Wanting-My-Love
All-You-Get – Instead
Is-Your-Head – Knocked-Off
By a Jagged-Board – That-I-Found

(Chorus)
You Come From A Nightmare
Stinking To Low Hell
Saying To Me – I Love You
Telling Me You're My One
In Deep Shock I Reply
You're Dead – I Can't Love You

253. She's Not Dead

I-Was so Happy – We-Finally-Made-It
Sold-Our-Company – For a Grand-Price
There-Was-Nothing – That-We-Could
Not-Do-Now – At-Last – We-Were-Free
To be Together – Living-Our-Lives in Peace

Tragedy – Took-My-Love – From-Me
Making-Me-Feel – Making-Me-Believe
That-Her-Death – Was-Not-Real
Everybody-Told-Me to Accept-This
That-She – Was-Gone-Forever
She-Was-Never – Coming-Back to Life

(Chorus)
She's Not Dead
She's Just Not Re-Alive Yet
With My Magic
She Will Live Once Again
Being With Me Forever

Searching-This-World – Trying to Find
Magic – That-Will-Bring-My
Dead-Love – Back to Life
Finding at First – Only-Nothing
Fake-Nothings – Full of Lies and Deceit
Wanting-Only – My-Money and Tears

Every-Once in Awhile
I-Find – Something-Special
Not-Enough – For-What-I-Need
None-The-Less a Person-With-Power
With-Each-New-Power – Taken-From-Them
I'm-One-Step-Closer to Finding-My-Way

(Chorus)
She's Not Dead
She's Just Not Re-Alive Yet
With My Magic
She Will Live Once Again
Being With Me Forever

22

Time is Now – I'm-Powered-Up – With-Magic
Feel-Like a God – Why-Not – Only a God-Can-Do
What-I'm-About to Do – Recreate-Life – From-No-Life
My-Dead-Love – You've-Been-Dead – Twenty-Years
I-Don't-Want to Wait – One-More-Minute
To be With-You – To-Hold-You – To-Kiss-You-Madly

Releasing-All-The-Power of Magic – Within-Me
Pointing-It at Your-Grave – With-Such-Force
Blows-Up-Your-Tombstone – Shifting-Your-Ground
Sending-Dirt and Grass – Into the Air – Catching-Fire
Voices of The-Dead – Warn-Me – What-I-Do
Is-Against the Law of Mother-Nature
If-I-Don't-Stop – She-Will-Make – Me-Pay

(Chorus)
She's Not Dead
She's Just Not Re-Alive Yet
With My Magic
She Will Live Once Again
Being With Me Forever

Laughing at Mother-Nature's – Warning of Doom
Watching-My-Dead-Love – Rise-Up-Alive
She-Walks to Me – Smiling so Lovingly
She-Kisses-Away – Years of Long-Lost
My-Alive-Love – Pulls-Back
Showing-Me-Huge – Demonic-Eyes and Teeth

With-No-Power-Left – I'm-Helpless
As-My-Love – Eats-My-Face – Off-My-Head
My-Love-Reaches – Down the Hole
She-Ate-Up and Pulls-Out-My-Soul
Taking-It-Back into The-Ground – With-Her
Leaving-My-Body to Rot-Away
To-Nothing-But – Lonely-Dust

(Chorus)
She's Not Dead
She's Just Not Re-Alive Yet
With My Magic
She Will Live Once Again
Being With Me Forever

254. Evil Love

Nice-Ladies – Bad-Ladies
Ladies-That-Say – Yes
Ladies-That-Say – No
They-Are-Out-There – Ready
To-Please and Not-Please-Me

I-Work-Hard or Not at All
Then-One – Sexy-Nightmare
There-She-Was – My-Evil-Love
My-Evil-Sexy – Lady of Pain

(Chorus)
Evil Love Is On My Back
Evil Love Is In My Sack
Evil Love Eats My Heart
Evil Love I Love Her
Evil Love I Hate Her
Would You Like To Try Her
She Will Rip Your Soul Out
Without One Bit Of Love Inside Her

Candle-Light and Bloody-Screams
Biting-Kisses – Evil-Ecstasy
My-Evil-Sexy-Lady of Pain
Tears at My-Flesh – She-Loves-It
It's-So-Sexy-Evil-Delicious

When-I-Tell – My-Evil-Love to Stop
She-Laughs and Bites-Down-Harder
When-I-Tell – My-Evil-Love – Not to Stop
She-Laughs and Makes-Me – Beg-For-More

(Chorus)
Evil Love Is On My Back
Evil Love Is In My Sack
Evil Love Eats My Heart
Evil Love I Love Her
Evil Love I Hate Her
Would You Like To Try Her
She Will Rip Your Soul Out
Without One Bit Of Love Inside Her

Can-You-Feel – My-Heartbeat
Baby it Beats so Fast-For-You
Love of Mine is Burning and Burning
Faster and Faster – Towards-Your-Heart

Baby-You're-My – All-That and More
My-Love is In-Your-Hands
Will-You be My-Angel – Will-You
Want-Me to Become – Your-Beast

(Chorus)
I Don't Know You
You're New To My Body
Yet You Now Own My Soul
You Smile And Smile
Making My Mind – Weaker And Weaker
As You – Teach Me How To Growl
Like A Good Beast – That's Under Your Control

Can-You-Feel – My-Heartbeat
Baby it Beats so Fast-For-You
May-I-Kiss-You – Please
Baby – Can-I-Be-Pleased
I've-Been a Good-Beast – I've-Done-My-Chores
It's-Now-My – Love-Love-Time

Baby-Why do You – Have to Punish-Me so Hard
Can't-You-Get – Turned-On – Without
Making-Me-Bleed-First – Am-I
Just-Your-Beast of Blood and Lust
Will-I-Ever-Be – Worthy of Your-Love

(Chorus)
I Don't Know You
Your New To My Body
Yet You Now Own My Soul
You Smile And Smile
Making My Mind – Weaker And Weaker
As You – Teach Me How To Growl
Like A Good Beast – That's Under Your Control

255. Satanic Lady Of The Night

Dated-Her – Banged-Her
Life-Never – Changes-Much
When-All-I-Have is Sexy
Golden-Angels to Sex-With

I-Want-Sexy-Evil – Underneath-Me
Tasting-My – Bleeding-Blood
Eating the Tips – Off-My-Wings
Turning-On – My-Angel-Body
That is Craving – Sexy-Evil-Hell-Lust

(Chorus)
Satanic Lady Of The Night
Hold Me So Tight
Satanic Lady Of The Night
Have A Feather From My Wings
Satanic Lady Of The Night
I Love Every Evil Part Of You
Satanic Lady Of The Night
Please Keep All The Good Away

Satanic-Lady of The-Night
Are-You – The-Devil's-Whore
Does-He – Know-About-Me
About-My-Angel-Hood – From-Heaven
That-Keeps-You – Flying-Back-For-More

You-Use-Me – I-Use-You-More
Now-Go-Back to Hell to Burn
While-I-Fly – Back to Heaven
Being-Punished – For-My-Weakness

(Chorus)
Satanic Lady Of The Night
Hold Me So Tight
Satanic Lady Of The Night
Have A Feather From My Wings
Satanic Lady Of The Night
I Love Every Evil Part Of You
Satanic Lady Of The Night
Please Keep All The Good Away

Rock And Roll Demon Man

Hello-Hottie – With a Twisted-Soul
Thought – I'd-Say-Hello
Since-You're – Going to Hell
After – You – Die

Why the Tears – Sexy-Evil-Hearted
You-Lead – Your-Lovers to Their-Deaths
Like a Spider – To a Fly
Don't-Worry-Hottie – It's-Cool-With-Me
Let's-Rock and Roll

(Chorus)
Evil Lady I'm The
Rock And Roll Demon Man
Come On Evil Lady
Let's Get Undressed
Evil Lady I'm The
Rock And Roll Demon Man
I've Come All The Way From Hell
To Have Sex With You First

Hottie-With a Twisted-Soul
Time to Say-Goodbye
You-Were-Great – I-Was-Better
Time for Your-Soul to Fall
All the Way to Un-Sweet-Hell

Why the Tears – Sexy-Evil-Hearted
You-Lead – Your-Lovers to Their-Deaths
Like a Spider to a Fly
Don't-Worry-Hottie – It's-Cool-With-Me
Let's-Rock and Roll

(Chorus)
Evil Lady I'm The
Rock And Roll Demon Man
Come On Evil Lady
Let's Get Undressed
Evil Lady I'm The
Rock And Roll Demon Man
I've Come All The Way From Hell
To Have Sex With You First
27

246. Lick The Blood Off Your Fingers

You-Look so Pale – My-Friend
Have-You-Been – Drinking-Enough-Blood
I-Thought-Not – What's the Matter
Blood-Doesn't-Taste – Good to You-Now

You-Have a Problem
With-Being a Vampire
I've-Had-Enough – Come-With-Me
You're-Going to Drink – Someone-Down – or
I'll-Kick – Your-Weak-Undead-Ass

(Chorus)
Blood Here – Blood There
You're A Vampire In The Night
Attack Attack – Drink Drink
All The Blood Humans Have To Offer
When You're Done Remember To
Lick The Blood Off Your Fingers

You're-Looking-Better – My-Friend
There's-Nothing-Like – Fresh-Blood
To-Make a Vampire – Feel-Replenished
Where the Hell – You-Going
You're-Not-Done – Drinking-Blood

Tonight is Still-Young and I'm-Hungry
Watching-You-Drink – That-Human-Down
Created-Such a Thirst-Inside-Me
Tell-You-What – My-Friend
You-Drink-One-More – Down-Tonight
While-I-Grab a Couple of Humans to
Drink-Down-With-You – I'll-Be-Right-Back

(Chorus)
Blood Here – Blood There
You're A Vampire In The Night
Attack Attack – Drink Drink
All The Blood Humans Have To Offer
When You're Done Remember To
Lick The Blood Off Your Fingers

247. Belly Full Of Blood

We've-Been-Friends for Years
Hundreds and Hundreds of Them
I-Have-Always – Told-You-This
That-You-Think too Much
With-Your-Heart and Not
Enough – With-Your-Fangs

This is The-Dead – Truth
Your-EX – Undead-Lady
Was-Nothing-But a Dirty-Slut
She-Even-Had-Sex – With-The-Living
So-My-Friend – I-Say-Forget-Her
Let's-Go-On a Blood-Binge

(Chorus)
That's It My Friend
Fill Your Very Hungry
Belly Full Of Blood
Drink Deep – Drink Them Dry
That's It My Friend
Keep On Filling Your
Belly Full Of Blood

Friend-I'm-Still-Thirsty – For-More-Blood
How-About-You – What-Do-You-Mean
You've-Had-Enough – Blood to Drink
Sun-Won't be Coming-Up – For a Few-More-Hours

Look-Over-There – That's-One-Tasty
Looking-Blood-Bag – If-I-Ever-Saw-One
Tell-You-What-My-Friend – Why-Don't-You
Sex-Her-First – Then-Drink-Her-Dry – Now-That-I
Think-About-It – Maybe-You-Just – Need to Get-Laid

(Chorus)
That's It My Friend
Fill Your Very Hungry
Belly Full Of Blood
Drink Deep – Drink Them Dry
That's It My Friend
Keep On Filling Your
Belly Full Of Blood

(Thirteen Witches With Thirteen Evil Sons: 248-250)

248. Thirteen Witches

Through-Fate – Thirteen-Ladies – A-Long-Time-Ago
Met-The-Other – During-Twelve-Day's-Time
The-Next-Night – The-Thirteenth-Night

With-Love in Their-Hearts
Freedom in Their-Minds
With-Peace in Their-Souls

They-Danced – They-Kissed – They-Shared
Their-Bodies – Loving-The-Thirteen of Them
Has-Now – Become-One

(Chorus #1)
Love Of Mother Earth – Love Of Womanhood
Thirteen Ladies – Become Thirteen Witches
Wanting Only To Live Together As One
Making This Forest The Most
Magical Place On Earth – For All
Women To Enter – To Become Sister Witches

Dancing – Psychedelic – Sensations
Darkness-All-Around – With-Only-The-Fire
To-Keep-Them-Safe – From-The-Forest

Thirteen-Witches – Keep-Dancing
Drinking-Wine – Eating-Mushrooms
Tossing-Green-Herbs – Into-The-Flames

Not-Caring – When a Magic-Man
Came-Alive – From-Out of The-Flames
Bringing-With-Him – His-Tainted-Lust

(Chorus #1)
Love Of Mother Earth – Love Of Womanhood
Thirteen Ladies – Become Thirteen Witches
Wanting Only To Live Together As One
Making This Forest The Most
Magical Place On Earth – For All
Women To Enter – To Become Sister Witches

One by One – The-Magic-Man – Tempts
Tastes and Enjoys – The-Thirteen-New-Witches
With-His-Evil-Laced – Magic-Manhood

The-Magic-Man's – Love-Talks – Is-Like-Nothing
The-New-Thirteen-Witches – Has-Ever-Heard
As 13 New-Witches – Loves-Their 13 Minutes of Ecstasy

169 Sex-Minutes-Later – The-Magic-Man-Leaves
Stepping-Back-Into-The-Flames – Without-Looking-Back
Leaving-Behind – 13 Sex-Hungry-New-Witches

(Chorus #2)
Love Of Mother Earth – Love Of Womanhood
Thirteen Ladies – Become Thirteen Witches
Wanting Only To Live Together As One
Wanting Nothing To Do Anymore With Mankind
With Their Forever – Lust – War And Death

Treat-Then-The-Trick for Thirteen-Witches
Nine-Full-Moons-Later – As-Thirteen-Witches
Are-Giving-Birth to Thirteen-New-Sons

Tears in Their-Eyes – They-Compare-Sons
Horror in Their-Hearts – They-Scream
For-All-Thirteen – Baby-Boys – Look-The-Same

Smoke-Then-Fire – The-Magic-Man – Reappears
Chanting and Laughing – He-Casts a Spell – Leaving-All
13 Witches-Paralyzed – Taking-With-Him – 13 New-Sons

(Chorus #2)
Love Of Mother Earth – Love Of Womanhood
Thirteen Ladies – Become Thirteen Witches
Wanting Only To Live Together As One
Wanting Nothing To Do Anymore With Mankind
With Their Forever – Lust – War And Death

249. Thirteen Evil Sons:
I. The Spell Of Protection
II. Die This Darkened Night

I. The Spell Of Protection

Thirteen-Years-Has-Passed – Since-That-First-Night
When-Thirteen-Witches – Became as One
The-Same-Night – All-Thirteen of Them
Were-Used by The-Magic-Man
Lusting-Them – Leaving-Behind – 13 Seeds

They-Felt-Blessed – Until-The-Night
The-Magic-Man-Returned and Stole-Their-Sons
Since-That-Night – Thirteen-Witches
Agreed as One – That-No-Man
Will-Ever-Use – Them-Again

(Chorus)
Magic Man You Evil Bastard
Give Us Back Our Thirteen Sons
We Hate You – We Will Find You
We Thirteen Witches
Will Make You Pay – For Your Evil Ways

Thirteen-Witches – Lived-Together in Harmony
They-Remember so Deeply – That-Night
That-They-Return – Thirteen-Years-Later
Casting a Spell of Protection – For-Their 13 Sons

(Chanting)
Our-Sons-We-Defend – From-Evil-Magic-Man's-Sin
Our-Sons-We-Shield – For-This-We-Will-Not-Yield
Our-Sons-We-Will-Keep – We-Will-Not-Follow-Like-Sheep
Our-Sons-You-We-Protect – Our-Love-Do-Not-Reject
Our-Sons-We-Defend – From-Evil-Magic-Man's-Sin
Come-Back-To-Your-Mothers – Reject-The-Evil-In-Your-Hearts

(Chorus)
Magic Man You Evil Bastard
Give Us Back Our Thirteen Sons
We Hate You – We Will Find You
We Thirteen Witches
Will Make You Pay – For Your Evil Ways

II. Die This Darkened Night

Look-Deep-Inside – The-Cauldron
See-What-Happened – One-Evil-Night
A-Very-Long-Time-Ago – To-Thirteen-Witches
Whose-Only-Crime – Was-Being-Themselves

The-Protection – Spell-Cast
Thirteen-Witches – Dry-Their-Crying-Eyes
Thirteen-Witches – Gather-For a Hug
13 Witches– Want to Leave – This-Dark-Forest-Behind

This is The-First-Time in Thirteen-Years
The-Thirteen-Witches – Have-Returned-Here
Then-Like a Bad-Omen – Smoke
Then-Fire – The-Magic-Man – Reappears

(Chorus)
Out Of The Flames Of Fire
Thirteen Stolen Sons Return
With Darkness Inside Their Souls
With Thirteen Years Of Evil Teachings
They Make Their Witch Mothers
Die This Darkened Night

Witches – You-Don't-Look the Same
Thirteen-Years – Have-Not-Been-Kind to You
Don't-Worry – Your-Pretty-Little – Witches'-Heads
Your-End – The-End of You-Thirteen-Witches
Has-Come to Be – On-This-Darkened-Night

I-Have-Brought-With-I – Your-Thirteen-Sons
Taught-Them-Well – Taught-Them to Hate and Kill
You 13 Witches – Should-Be so Proud of My 13 Sons
Look-Into-Their-Eyes – See in Them – Their-Dark-Souls
Souls so Dark – That-They-Can't-Wait – To-Kill-All 13 of You

(Chorus)
Out Of The Flames Of Fire
Thirteen Stolen Sons Return
With Darkness Inside Their Souls
With Thirteen Years Of Evil Teachings
They Make Their Witch Mothers
Die This Darkened Night

33

250. The Curse / The Rise Of The 13th Witch

The Curse

Twelve-Witches – Lie-Dead on The-Ground
Thirteenth-Witch – Bleeding to Death
From-Wounds – Given to Her by Her-Son
With-Her-Last-Words – Spoken-Out – She-Curses
The-Magic-Man and His-Thirteen-Evil-Sons

Thirteen-Years – From-This-Night
I-Will be Re-Born to Un-Dead-Life
I-Will-Seek – All-Fourteen of You-Out
Enjoy-Your-Victory – You-Evil-Men
When-We-Meet-Again – In-Thirteen-Years
I-Will-Rip-Off-Your-Flesh and Eat-Your-Souls to Death

(Chorus)
Thirteen Evil Sons And One Magic Man
Almost Laughed Their Souls Out Of Themselves
From Hearing The Curse Of The Thirteenth Witch
Then They Picked Up Her Dead Body
Along With The Other Twelve Dead Witches
Throwing Them All In A Pit And Setting Them On Fire

(Repeat Chorus)

The Rise Of The 13th Witch

The-Night-Before-The-End of The-Thirteen-Year-Curse
The-Magic-Man – Has a Vision – And a Dream
His-Life-Taken by The-Thirteenth-Witch
Very-Evil-Wise and Never a Fool to Take-Chances
The-Magic-Man-Leaves – His-Thirteen-Evil-Sons
Behind-The-Next-Morning – Without a Warning

Night-Falls – With-Vicious-Storms in The-Sky
Thirteen-Evil-Sons – Beg-For-Their-Evil-Father
Left-Alone-Without-Protection – They-Scatter
From-The-Storm – Away-From-The-Curse
Of-The-Unforgiving – Thirteenth-Witch

(Chorus)
Run – Run Like Cowards
You Evil Born – Thirteen Sons
From The Coming Curse Of The
The Rise Of The 13th Witch
Your Blood – Death And Souls
I Will Feast On This Night

Like a Vengeance – Unseen on Earth
With-Mother-Earth's – Blessing
The 13th Witch – Rises-From-Death
No-Longer a Care-Free and Loving-Witch
Now-She's an Un-Dead – Rage-For-Vengeance

The 13th Witch – Laughs and Flies-Into-The-Storm
She-Seeks-Out and Finds – The-13-Evil-Sons
One by Bloody-One – They-Die-Hard
One by Bloody-One – They-Die – Screaming to Death

With 13 Evil-Sons' – Blood on Her-Hands
The 13th Witch – Screams at The-Night
I'm-Coming-For-You – Evil-Magic-Man
Your-Blood – Will-Flow-Free-Upon – My-Hands

(Chorus)
Run – Run Like Cowards
You Evil Born – Thirteen Sons
From The Coming Curse Of The
The Rise Of The 13th Witch
Your Blood – Death And Souls
I Will Feast On This Night

The-Sun is Rising in The-Morning-Sky
All-Night-Long – The 13th Witch
Searched for The-Magic-Man
But to No-Avail – He-Hid so Very-Well

With-Intense-Anger – The 13th Witch
Curses-The-Magic-Man – One-More-Time
This-Same-Night-Next-Year – I-Will be Re-Born
Every-Year-After-That – Until-You-Die by My-Hands
You-Evil – Magic-Man – Evil-Bastard

(Repeat Chorus)
35

Evil Lady (425.)

I-Never-Had – Any-Trouble
Always-Some-Lady – Out-There
Always – Willing to Give-Me
What-I-Want and Need

Then-They're – Holding-My-Hand
Telling-Me – They're a Nice-Lady
That-They're – Looking-For-Love
Not-Having-Sex – With-Someone
Waiting to Just – Say-Goodbye
When-They-Had – Enough of Her

I'm so Down on Ladies
Looking-Just for Love
I'm-Still-Up – For a Lady
Wanting-Only – One-Thing

(Chorus)
Evil Lady Why Don't You
Come Sit Down Beside Me
I've Tried Enough Nice Ladies
Now I Want To Know What
Your Evilness Can Do For Me

You-Walk-By so Slowly
Dressed-In-Black
With-Skin – Very-Pale-White
You-Look at Me and Hiss
Something-Happens – In-My-Pants
As-My-Heart-Turns – Towards-The-Dark

I-Say to You – I-Think-I'm
Finally-Falling in Lust
About – Damn – Time
I-Knew-Love – Was-Good
I-Just-Didn't-Know – I-Was-Evil
That's-Why – I-Always-Hated-It

Evil-Lust – With an Evil-Lady
Is so Much-More – Of a Release
I-Tell-You-What – Nice-Ladies
If-I-Got-The-Time and You're-Fine
One-Night – With-My-Evilness
I'll-Turn-You – Into a Evil-Lady
So-You-Can – Help-Spread
Evil-Lust – Around-This-World

(Chorus)
Evil Lady Why Don't You
Come Sit Down Beside Me
I've Tried Enough Nice Ladies
Now I Want To Know What
Your Evilness Can Do For Me

Evil Lady Why Don't You
Come Sit Down On Top Of Me
I Want To Feel – Turned On By Evil
I'll Let You Have Your Turn
Then I'll Have Mine – Drop You Behind
On My Way To – World Wide Evil Lusting

(Bonus Song)

Hello Lady Of Death (553.)

Lady of Death – Has-Always
Watched-Me – Growing-Up
She-Would-Entice-Me

Appearing-Only – Long-Enough
That-I-Felt-Her
Sweet – Death – Embrace
For a Fleeting-Moment
I-Loved-It so Much

(Chorus)
Hello Lady Of Death
You Are So Beautiful
May I Kiss Your Lips
Hello Lady Of Death
I Want To Taste Your Death
37

I-Have to Own-Her
My-Lady of Death
No-Other-Man – Can-Have-Her
She is All-Mine to Love

I-Know – She-Loves-Me
She-Tells – Me-This
So-Many – Loving-Times
Foreplay is Over – Tonight
I'm-Getting-My – Death-Kiss

(Chorus)
Hello Lady Of Death
You Are So Beautiful
May I Kiss Your Lips
Hello Lady Of Death
I Want To Taste Your Death

I-Beg – My-Lady of Death
For-My – Death-Kiss
She-Brings-Her – Cold-Blue-Lips
Over to Mine and Kills-Me

I-Appear – Above-My-Body
It's-Dead – I'm so Happy
I-Can-Now – Fully-Own
My-Lady of Death
She-Smiles at Me – With-Hate
Shoves-Me – Into a Burning-Hole
That-Leads – All-The-Way to Hell

(Chorus)
Hello Lady Of Death
You Are So Beautiful
May I Kiss Your Lips
Hello Lady Of Death
I Want To Taste Your Death

La – La – La – Lady of Death
The-Lady – I-Love-Best
La – La – La – Lady of Death
The-Lady – I-Tried to Own
La – La – La – Lady Of Death
The-Lady-That-Makes – Your-Soul-Burn

38

Book Fourteen: Gemini Beast (Pages 39-77)

(Side One)
261. The Gemini Beast (667.)
262. Feast With The Beasties (465.)
     Blood Beast **(813.)**
263. Come On Over To Me (29.)
264. Demons Are Living On Earth (599.)
     Paint Death **(836.)**
265. Beast Of Men Running Amok (349.)

(Side Two)
266. Mary And Lizzy Likes Blood (560.)
267. Lust Feast & Lust Feast (Stained In Blood) (555.)
268. The Dead Lady Kissed Me (755.)
269. Screaming Sally (112.)
270. Cannibal Butcher (460.)

(Side Three)
271. They Live In Darkness (556.)
272. Total Darkness And Pain (575.)
     Grave Of Doom **(809.)**
273. Here Comes Hell (619.)
274. Hell's Metal Monster (402.)
275. Death-Angels (Wings Of Steel) (797.)

(Side Four)
276. When The Aliens Attack (309.)
277. Get Off That Damn Space Alien (513.)
(Evil Magic Wizard Wants A Son Trilogy: 278-280)
278. Young Lust Turns To Dead Love (743.)
279. What Is A Evil Wizard To Do (744.)
280. Growing Up Evil (In Three Parts) (745.)
     I. Nice And Evil At Thirteen
     II. Dating With Evil Inside Her
     III. Lady Evil Is All Alone

(Bonus Songs)
What Is Evil (Sweat In Hell) (568.)
Vampire Kiss (I Drink, You Lust) (552.)
Vampire Kiss Baby (I Drink, You Suck) **(Demo)**

261. The Gemini Beast

Created a Long-Time-Ago
Before – There-Was-Sin
Gods-Came-Along – With-Fury
After-Being – Questioned by Their
Angels – That-They-Created

Questions of Why
One-Time-Too-Many
Angered the We – That is One
Lucifer-Paid – The-Price
Becoming-The-Ruler of Hell
Let's-Have-Some-Fun
While-Hearing-From-Satan

(Chorus)
I'm The Gemini Beast
Come Sin With Me
Taste My Hell Fire
As I Make It Bleed
I'm The Gemini Beast
Come Sin With Me
Die And Burn In Hell
As I Lust And Slaughter

Lucifer-The-Grand
Now-The-Fallen-One
Being-Transformed – Into-The-Beast
In a Giant-Bubbling – Stinking-Pit
Filled-With-Evil and Hate

The-Grandness – That-Lies-In
Lucifer's-Being – The-One-That-Loves
Love-And-Peace – Is-Not-Being-Destroyed
It's-Being – Pushed-Aside

Making-Room – For-Mayhem
Chaos in Burning-Flesh
Let's-Have-Some-Fun
While-Hearing-From-Satan

(Chorus)
I'm The Gemini Beast
Come Sin With Me
Taste My Hell Fire
As I Make It Bleed
I'm The Gemini Beast
Come Sin With Me
Die And Burn In Hell
As I Lust And Slaughter

What is Your-Price – Man
Fame and Fortune
What is Your-Price – Lady
Youth and Beauty
Both – I-Can-Grant – Right-Now
All it Cost is Your-Soul

I-Do-Not-Lie – Maybe a Little
When-I-Tell-You – That-God
Does-Not – Love-You
But on The-Hell – Side of It
Neither-Do-I – I-Hate-You

It's-Hard to Love – Something
That-Is so Human and Flawed
Do-Not-Dread – Scum
At-Least-You – Have-Souls
That-Are-Worthless to You
Until of Course – You-Die
Then-I-Get – First-Crack at Them

(Chorus)
I'm The Gemini Beast
Come Sin With Me
As I Make It Bleed
Or Die And Burn In Hell
I'm The Gemini Beast
Come Sin With Me
As I Lust And Slaughter
Or Die And Burn In Hell

41

262. Feast With The Beasties

It's-Friday-The 13th – Night-Time – Play-Time
We're-Going to Have a Bash
And-Not-Take – Out-The-Trash
Bottles of Whiskey – Cracked-Wide-Open
Kegs of Beers – Tapped and Pumping

Plenty of Fresh-Humans
For-Us-Beasties to Eat-Up
Some of Us-Beasties – Like-To-Go
All-The-Way – We-Like to Play
With-Our – Human-Meals
We-Kiss and Make-Sex
With-The-Ones – That-We're
Going to Be-Eating – Later

(Chorus)
Party Time For The Humans
As They Get All Trashed Up
Never Knowing Before It's
Way Too Late To Run Away
That They Foolishly Entered
A Feast With The Beasties

Dawn-Will be Breaking – Soon
All-Our-Beasties – Bellies-Are-Full
We-Use-Finger-Bones – Lying-Around
To-Pick-Our – Beastly-Human
Chunk-Filled-Teeth – Clean

We-Walk-Away – Before
It-Becomes – Too-Bright
We'll be Long-Gone
Before-The-Sun – Shines-Down-On
The-Bone-Filled – Slaughter-Ground

(Chorus)
Party Time For The Humans
As They Get All Trashed Up
Never Knowing Before It's
Way Too Late To Run Away
That They Foolishly Entered
A Feast With The Beasties

Blood Beast

Did-God – Create-It
No – He-Did-Not
Did-Mother-Earth – Create-It
No – She-Did-Not
Did-Mankind – Create-It
Hell-Yeah – They-Did

Stupid – Ass – Idiots
Cannot-Leave – Well-Enough-Alone
Stupid – Ass – Idiots
Had to Prove – They-Could-Do-It
Stupid – Ass – Idiots
Created-The-Blood-Beast

(Chorus)
Run Like Hell Man
The Blood Beast – The Blood Beast
Is Coming This Way – It Will
Leave You With – Your Flesh And Bones
As It Drinks Away – All Your Blood

Did-God – Create-It
No – He-Did-Not
Did-Mother-Earth – Create-It
No – She-Did-Not
Did-Mankind – Create-It
Hell-Yeah – They-Did

Stupid – Ass – Idiots
Cannot-Leave – Well-Enough-Alone
Stupid – Ass – Idiots
Had to Prove – They-Could-Do-It
Stupid – Ass – Idiots
Created the Blood-Beast

(Chorus)
Run Like Hell Man
The Blood Beast – The Blood Beast
Is Coming This Way – It Will
Leave You With – Your Flesh And Bones
As It Drinks Away – All Your Blood

263. Come On Over To Me

I-Know-About – The-Father
Son and Holy-Ghost
Come on Over to Me
I'll-Show-You – The-Light
I'll-Even – Hold-On to Your
Wallet – When-You-Are-Gone

Just-Call – My-Hot-Line
One of Many – Trucks
Can-Take-All – That-You-Have-Away
I'll-Keep-Taking and Taking
Laughing-All-The-Way to The-Bank
Keeping-The-Profits so Clean
No-Taxes – I-Ever-Need to Pay

(Chorus)
Come On Over To Me
I'll Be Your Savior
Don't Matter That I'm Lying
You'll Keep Giving To Me
I'll Take Your Money
For My Church – For My God
So Come On Over To Me
Pay Me Thickly My Faithful
If You Want To Go To Heaven

Don't-You-Wish – You-Were-Me
Spreading-The-Word of God
Raking-In – All-That-Dough
The-More-Homes and Cars – That-I-Have
Makes it Easier – For-Me to Get to You

When-You-Come to Bask in My-Splendor
Don't-Forget to Fill-Up – My-Plates-Full
Before-You-Leave – If-You-Don't-Understand
What-I-Am – Then-You-Truly – Don't-Believe
You-Are-Not-Worth – Saving
I'll-See to It – That-God-Makes – You-Burn

(Repeat Chorus)

44

To-All-My – Faithful-Flock
Continue-Your-Belief in Me
Give-Me-Everything – You-Have
You'll be Fine – With-Naught
While-God and I – Are-Rich and Fat

You-Are-Such – Good-Mindless-Sheep
If-You-Walk – Away-From-Me
You-Will-Burn – Forever in Hell
There-Will-Be – No-Hope-For-You
How-Do-I – Know-This
Simple – God-Tells-Me-This
So-Keep on Listening
Obeying and Giving – All-Your-Money to Me

(Chorus)
Come On Over To Me
I'll Be Your Savior
Don't Matter That I'm Lying
You'll Keep Giving To Me
I'll Take Your Money
For My Church – For My God
So Come On Over To Me
Pay Me Thickly My Faithful
If You Want To Go To Heaven

What's-That – You-Have-No-More
Money to Give to Me
Well-Then – You-Must go Away
You-Can-Not be Saved
You're-Still-Here – Hell-No
I-Don't-Have-Anything to Give to You
What do You-Think – I'm a Charity

You-Want-God – You-Pay-For-It
He's-Not-For-Free
That's-The – Poor-Man's-God
With-The-Bankrupt – Heaven
Nothing-But-Garbage to See
No-Way is That-For-Me
God and I – Are-Super-Clean

(Repeat Chorus)

264. Demons Are Living On Earth

Flash of Light
Crash of Thunder
Death-From – The-Sky
Evil-Eyes – Squirting-Bloody-Fire
I-Fear – This-Dark-Night

Where-Can-I – Run to
My-Soul is The-Prize
Demons-With-Long – Fangs and Claws
With-Razor and Barbwire-Wings
Want to Eat – My-Soul-Out of Me

(Chorus)
God Where The Hell Are You
Demons Are Living On Earth
Eating Up All Our Souls To Death
If It's Not Too Much Trouble
Could You Smite Them All Away
Thank You So Very – Damn Much

Demons on My-Back
Slashing at Me – With-Their-Claws
While-Their – Soul-Eating-Teeth
Chomp-Together in Devouring-Ways
I'm so Tired – I-Hate-My-Life

Nothing is Left – Inside-Myself
Fear-The-Pain – I-Will-Receive
My-Chest – Ripped-Apart to Shreds
Soul-Inside-Me – Like-Candy to These
Demons-That-Love to Kill-All-Humans

(Chorus)
God Where The Hell Are You
Demons Are Living On Earth
Eating Up All Our Souls To Death
If It's Not Too Much Trouble
Could You Smite Them All Away
Thank You So Very – Damn Much

Paint Death

Dying-World – You-Look so Pretty
Please-Please – More-Blood-Slaughter
I-Crave-It so Much

Thank-You – Thank-You
You-Are so Kind and Helpful
Mankind-You-Make – The-World so Evil

(Chorus)
Paint Death – Paint Death
Such A Pretty Color
Paint Death – Paint Death
With A Smile On Your Face
Paint Death – Paint Death
Keep On Painting – 'Til You Are All Dead

Dead-Souls – You-Look so Ugly
Please-Please – Stay-Away
You-Have – No-More-Worth

Thank-You – Thank-You
You-Were so Easy and Stupid
Mankind-You-Made – The-World-All-Dead

(Chorus)
Paint Death – Paint Death
Such A Pretty Color
Paint Death – Paint Death
With A Smile On Your Face
Paint Death – Paint Death
Keep On Painting – 'Til You Are All Dead

Call-Me-Lucifer – I-Never-Lie – I-Always-Lie
Call-Me-Lucifer – I-Live-In-Hell – I-Am-King
I-Have-The-Best-Stuff – This-Side-Of-Heaven
Love-Me – Hate-Me – I-Need-Only-One-Scratch
Call-Me-Lucifer – I-Never-Lie – I-Always-Lie
Call-Me-Lucifer – I-Live-In-Hell – I-Am-King
Glad-We-Were-Friends – Had-Such a Great-Time
Welcome to Hell-Everybody
Ready – Scream – Bleed and Burn
(Repeat Chorus)
47

265. Beast Of Men Running Amok

Night is Coming-Fast
Taking-Away – The-Last-Bit of
Frozen-Sun-From-Us
We-Can-Hear – The-Screams
Coming-From – The-North
Where-Snow and Ice – Take-Over

The-Beasts-That – Resemble-Man
Are-Coming to Devour-Us
We-Are-Cold – Starving
So-Very-Tired – This-Constant
Running is Killing-Us-Slowly
Day by Fearful-Day

(Chorus)
The World Has Changed
Right Before Our Eyes
Beasts Of Men Running Amok
Killing And Eating
Every Human They Find
Saving Some Of The Women
For Breeding Stock

Every-Beast – Can-Die
It's-Fact-These – Beast-Men-Are
Very-Very – Hard to Kill
They-Don't – Hunt-Alone
You-See-One – You-Don't-See-Twenty

Giant-Twelve-Feet-Tall
Eight-Hundred-Pounds – of
Killing and Eating
Ugly-Ass – Fast-Feasting
Never-Running-Out of Three-Inch
Fangs to Gut – Mangle – and
Eat-You-Down to The-Bone
With-No-Mercy – In-Them at All

(Chorus)
The World Has Changed
Right Before Our Eyes
Beasts Of Men Running Amok
Killing And Eating
Every Human They Find
Saving Some Of The Women
For Breeding Stock

When-We-Have – The-Time to Talk
We-Don't-Talk – About-The-Past
About-God and The-Devil
No-We-Don't – What's-The-Point
We-All-Know – This as Truth
There is No-God in Heaven

If-There is Then to Hell – With-God
For-He's a Sorry-Ass-God
That-Lets-Demons – Have-Free-Reign
Over-Us – Weak and Humble
Human-Beings of Earth

What-Do-We – Talk-About
You-Like to Know
We-Talk-About – The-Only
Four-Things – That-Ever-Matter
Surviving – Eating – Sleeping and Sex

(Chorus)
The World Has Changed
Right Before Our Eyes
Beasts Of Men Running Amok
Killing And Eating
Every Human They Find
Saving Some Of The Women
For Breeding Stock

266. Mary And Lizzy Likes Blood

Don't-Say – Mary's-Name
Three-Times in The-Dark
Turn on The-Lights
Then-Look-Into a Mirror

She'll be Waiting-For-You
On-The-Other-Side of The-Mirror
Since-You – Called-For-Her
She is Allowed to Eat-Your-Soul
Killing-You In The-Process

(Chorus)
Mary And Lizzy Likes Blood
They Were Forced To Kill
While They Were Alive
Mary And Lizzy Likes Blood
They Were Oppressed By Man
Now They Are Cursed To Burn In Hell

Don't-Say – Lizzy's-Name
Or – Give-Me-Forty-Whacks
If-You-Are-Alone – And a Man
While-Swinging an Axe

Lizzy-Hates – Her-Rhymes
It-Drives-Her – Blood-Swinging-Crazy
Your-Axe-Will-Appear – In-Her-Hands
Then-She'll-Chop-You to Pieces
With-Forty-One-Whacks

(Chorus)
Mary And Lizzy Likes Blood
They Were Forced To Kill
While They Were Alive
Mary And Lizzy Likes Blood
They Were Oppressed By Man
Now They Are Cursed To Burn In Hell

Mary and Lizzy – Have-Become-Friends
Since-They – Met in Hell
Girl-Talk – Turned-Into a Plan
On-How to Get-Out of Hell
And-Have a Murdering – Great-Time

Sweet-Talking – The-Devil-Was-Easy
Satan's-Always – Busy-Having-Fun
With-His – Torturing of Souls
To-Pay too Much-Attention

To a Couple of His-Best
Female-Demon – Soul-Eaters
Wanting to Go to Earth – Having a
Blood-Slaughtering – Great-Time

(Chorus)
Mary And Lizzy Likes Blood
They Were Forced To Kill
While They Were Alive
Mary And Lizzy Likes Blood
They Were Oppressed By Man
Now They Are Cursed To Burn In Hell

(Chorus)
Mary And Lizzy Likes Blood
They Were Forced To Kill
While They Were Alive
Mary And Lizzy Likes Blood
They Were Oppressed By Man
Now They Are Cursed To Burn In Hell

267. Lust Feast & Lust Feast (Stained In Blood)

Spin-The-Bottle – Key-Parties – Game of Smiles
Midnight-Quickies – In-The-Wet-Night
Love-Is-In-The-Air so Is-The-Smell of Sex
Been a Long-Time-Coming
For-This-Lust-Feast to Take-Off
Its-Clothes – And-Get to Moaning and Groaning

Sex-Appetites – Are-Quenched
Sharing-That – Someone-Special
Panties-Being – Given-Away
Bras-Thrown – Into-The-Bonfire
People-That-Don't – Know-The-Other
Having-Sexy – Fun-Together

(Chorus)
Lust Feast
Tonight All Night
Lust Feast
Bring Your Manhood
Bring Your Womanhood
And Get To Lusting

Whiskey and Lipstick – Candles and Oils
Two-Ladies for One-Man – Two-Men for One-Lady
There is No-Wrong or Right
This-Is a Lust Feast
For-The-Totally-Free
That-Like to Smile – With-Their-Clothes-Off

If-You-Can't – Get-It-Up
It's-Okay to Just-Watch
That's-Part of The-Lust-Feast-Rules
But it Can't-Compare to Joining-In
Having a Great – Lust-Feast-Time

(Chorus)
Lust Feast
Tonight All Night
Lust Feast
Bring Your Manhood
Bring Your Womanhood
And Get To Lusting
52

(Turns Into: Lust Feast – Stained in Blood)

Lust in The-Air – Brings-Out a Murderer
A-Being so Twisted – That-He'd-Rather-Kill
Than-Have-Sex – Lust-Feast-Style
Monster-Came-Out of The-Woods
Started-Shooting – Naked-Lust
Feast-People to Their-Bloody-Deaths

Their-Embrace – Became-Their-Last
As-This-Murdering – Monster
Kept-Firing-Away – With a Smile
The-Body-Count is Piling-Up
Because-He-Has so Many-Bullets

(Chorus)
Lust Feast – Stained In Blood
One Gun Wielding Lunatic
And A Whole Bunch Of Naked
Lust Feast – Dying People

Mr.-Murder is In-Ecstasy
The-Dirty-Bastard – Dirtying-His-Shorts
Rapid-Fire – Killing-Death
He-Won't-Stop-Shooting – Until
He-Runs-Out of Bullets

Faces – Ripped – Apart
Hearts – Stop – Beating
Tits and Pricks – On-The-Ground
All-This-Could – Have-Been-Stopped
By-Keeping-Guns-Away
From-Lunatics and Keeping
Lust-Feast-People – Free and Protected
While-They – Lust-Feast-Around

(Chorus)
Lust Feast – Stained In Blood
One Gun Wielding Lunatic
And A Whole Bunch Of Naked
Lust Feast – Dying People

268. The Dead Lady Kissed Me

I-Prayed to God but He
Never-Showed – His-Face
So-I-Said – Forget-This-Heavy
And-Went-Out and Got-Laid

Life-Was so Good at One-Time
Head-High in Fine-Ladies
Then-One – Midnight-Hour
There-She-Was – All-Dead and Gone
Wanting to Get a Hold of Somebody
To-Make-Her-Feel – Alive and Loved

(Chorus)
We Hugged – We Danced
Then The Dead Lady Kissed Me
The Maggots In Her Mouth – Tasted Sweet
Her Cold Lips Were So Soft
We Kissed And We Kissed
Then I Alive Rocked Her World
Only To Chop Her Into Pieces
When I Was Done – Because
Dead Ladies – Belong In The Ground

Life-Was so Good at One-Time
Head-High in Fine-Ladies
Then-One – Midnight-Hour
There-She-Was – All-Dead and Gone
Wanting to Get a Hold of Somebody
To-Make-Her-Feel – Alive and Loved

(Chorus)
We Hugged – We Danced
Then The Dead Lady Kissed Me
The Maggots In Her Mouth – Tasted Sweet
Her Cold Lips Were So Soft
We Kissed And We Kissed
Then I Alive Rocked Her World
Only To Chop Her Into Pieces
When I Was Done – Because
Dead Ladies – Belong In The Ground

269. Screaming Sally

Poor-Sally – Was-Used too Much
Guys-Would – Pick-Her-Up – Maybe-Feed-Her
Most-Definitely – Got-Their-Good-Time
Sally-Tried-Saying-No – Everybody-Knew-She
Had-No-Control – Such an Easy-Yes
Sally-Would-Never – Admit
This is Actually – What-She-Wanted

Moaning-Sally – Was-Known-As
The-Good-Time-Girl – When-You're-Horny
Go-Pick-Up-Sally and She'll-Let-You
But-One-Night – Sally-Had-Enough
After a Date – Got-Him-Some
Then-Rushed to Put on His-Clothes
When-Sally-Was-Expecting – Some-Cuddling
Guy-Didn't-Even – Want to Kiss-Her-Goodbye

(Chorus)
Screaming Sally – Is Man's Worst Friend
She Hates You – Wants To Eat You
She's A Crazy Hungry – Cannibal Lady
That Always Starts – By Biting Off Your Pecker

Stories-Are-Told of The-Night-When
Moaning-Sally-Became – Screaming-Sally
She-Grabbed – Up a Lamp
Bashed-This-Poor – Fool's-Head-In
Pulled-Down – His-Pants-And
Ate-His-Pecker – Right-Off-Him

Guys-Should-Remember – Sally's-Story
When-They-Go-Out to Find a Quickie
Lady-You're-Lusting – This-Night
Might-Have-Had – Enough of The-Same
Deciding to Follow – Sally's-Lead – Turning
Your-Pecker – Into a Hot-Dog – With-No-Bun

(Chorus)
Screaming Sally – Is Man's Worst Friend
She Hates You – Wants To Eat You
She's A Crazy Hungry – Cannibal Lady
That Always Starts – By Biting Off Your Pecker

55

270. Cannibal Butcher

You're a Sorry-Bastard
I-Hate-You so Much
Why-Don't-You – Kill-Me-Already
Stop-Torturing-Me
You-Don't-Want to Know-Anything
You-Don't – Ask-Me-Anything

You-Just-Slice – Off-My-Meat
Laughing – While-You're-Doing-It
Smelling-My-Meat – Being-All
Cooked-Up to Its-Most – Tasty-Perfection
Has-Made-Me – Lose-My-Mind

(Chorus)
You're My Cannibal Butcher
As You Slice Off My Meat To Eat
Laughing With A Way Up Too Close
Nasty Ass Smelling Mouth
That I'd Like To Kick You In
If I Ever Get The Chance

I-Talk – To a Stranger
I-Created – For-My-Sanity
As-This-Cannibal-Butcher – Works-Out-His
Very-Sick – Eating-Disorder on Me
I'm-Almost – All-Cooked-Up
Don't-Know-How – I'm-Still-Alive

This-Cannibal-Butcher – Is a Master-Maniac
I-Moan for Limbs – That-Are-No
Longer-There – With-My-Last-Thought
I-Laugh – Hoping-This-Cannibal-Butcher
Chokes to Death on The-Last of My-Meat

(Chorus)
You're My Cannibal Butcher
As You Slice Off My Meat To Eat
Laughing With A Way Up Too Close
Nasty Death Smelling Mouth
That I'd Like To Kick You In
If I Ever Get The Chance

271. They Live In Darkness

Come-Meet-The-Darkness – It-Will-Give-You
Such a Fright – What-You-Can't-Imagine
Coming to Bloody – Dark-Life
Running – Will do You – No-Good
You've-Tasted-Darkness – It-Likes-You
So-Much – That it Wants to Eat – Your-Soul

Darkness is Not a Sin – It's a Dark-Reality
That-Feeds-Off the Weak – Like a Void of
Dark-Parasites – Tenderizing-Its
Food-Source to Lushest-Bites
Love is Not the Answer – Darkness
Can't-Feel-It – It-Feels-Only-Hate
Hate-That-Will-Consume – Raw and Broken
In-Beautiful – Individual – Bloody-Pieces

(Chorus)
Pay Attention To
The Succubus And The Demon
They Live In The Darkness
Waiting To Spread It Around
Like Fire – To A Mortal Soul

Waving a Bible-Around – When-Darkness
Calls for You – Only-Causes-You-Pain
Your-Bible – Soaked in Your-Blood
The-Wizard and the Witch-Doctor
Could-Help-You – If-They-Cared to
They-Have-Their-Own – Problems to Worry-About
Than-Those – Who-Can-Not be Saved

(Chorus)
Pay Attention To
The Succubus And The Demon
They Live In The Darkness
Waiting To Spread It Around
Like Fire – To A Mortal Soul

Welcome to Darkness
It's-Forever and Always
Eternal and Wonderful – and
You're-Just a Simple-Meal

272. Total Darkness And Pain

Winds of Change – Are-Calling
Don't-Want to Answer-Them
I-Know-The-Pain – I-Will-Receive
Will-Rip and Burn – My-Soul-Apart

I-Like to Laugh
I-Like to Make-Love
Having-Drinks
Talking-Closely-Together
The-Touch of My-Love
Will be Taken – Away-From-Me

Staring at The-Sun
Love-It so Much
I-Don't-Want to Hate – The-Day
And-Bring-Forth – Total-Night
That is Forever – Fire and Death

Damn-This-All – I-Hate-You-Father
Your-Demons – Are so Sick and Vile
I-Want to Kill – Them-All – Before
They-Can – Breathe-Out – All-Their
Demon-Plague-Winds – Upon Earth

(Chorus)
I Can't Fight It – I'm The Devil's Son
That Was Bred To Be – Total Darkness And Pain
I Can't Fight It – I'm The Devil's Son
That Was Bred To Be – Total Darkness And Pain

I-Stand-Tall and Evil
Fighting for The-Rights of Hell
Satan-Wants to Come-Home
Caring-About – Nothing-Else
But the Pearly-Gates of Heaven

I'm-His-Tool – His-Puppet-Monster
Doing-What – He-Can't-Do
For-Satan – Can-Not-Leave-Hell
Until-He-Gets – The-Word-God
Will-One-Day – Give to Him

58

My-Mission – My-Father's-Orders
Kill and Destroy – Mankind
I-Said-No – He-Took-Away – My-Power
Sent-His-Demons to Slap-Me-Around
I-Took-The-Pain – Becoming-Stronger

Satan – Screams in Hell
Causing – Tidal-Waves of Fire
For-My-Constant – Defiance
Father-Hates-Me as Much as His-Hell
Now-He-Wants-Me to Come-Home
So-We-Can – Have a Nice-Talk

(Chorus)
I Can't Fight It – I'm The Devil's Son
That Was Bred To Be – Total Darkness And Pain
I Can't Fight It – I'm The Devil's Son
That Was Bred To Be – Total Darkness And Pain

Hell-Stinks and so Does-Satan
He is No – Nice-Father
As-He-Beats-Me – With-Hell's-Fire
I-Take-It and Take-It – Screaming-No
Satan-Laughs and Says – Play-Time is Over

Satan – Can-Bring-On-The-Pain
Finally-Having-Enough of Me – His-Son
He-Rips-Out-My-Soul and Eats-It
I-Don't-Love – Earth-Any-More
I-Just-Love – Fire and Brimstone

Attacking the Earth – With-My-Evil
It-Crumbles – Like-Old-Clay
Between-My-Fingers and Under-My-Feet
No-Tears – No-Remorse – No-Love
I'm-Just-Evil – Filled-With-Hell

Running-Free – Destroying-Everything
I'm-Slapped-Off – My-Fiery-Feet
Looking-Up-Seeing – God's-Giant-Foot
Coming-Down-Upon-Me – Squishing-Me to Death
Sending-Me – Straight to Hell – As a Failure to Father

(Repeat Chorus)

Grave Of Doom

Cut-Open – Wide and Bleeding
Meat-Market – Has-Your-Body
That-Died – While-Having-Sex
Heart-Attack – Just-Like-That
Without a Great-Big-Hurrah
Saving-You-From – This-Dying-Day

You're-Not-Special – You're-Just-Next
Let's-Hear – What-The-Dead – Had to Say

(Chorus)
I'm So Afraid To Die
Grave Of Doom
In The Back Of My Mind
Is It Going To Be Today
Is It Going To Be Tomorrow
I Just Can't Live This Way
Grave Of Doom – Grave Of Doom
Go Haunt Someone Else's Mind
With Your Doom Of Death And Grave

Worms-Wiggling – In-Your-Eyes
Maggots-Crawling – In-Your-Mouth
Death of An-Average-Human
Tossed in The-Ground-Cold
Without-Anyone to Cry-Any-Tears
Not-Even – The-Person-Unnamed
Whom-You-Died – Having-Sex-With

You're-Not-Special – You're-Just-Next
Let's-Hear – What-The-Dead – Had to Say

(Chorus)
I'm So Afraid To Die
Grave Of Doom
In The Back Of My Mind
Is It Going To Be Today
Is It Going To Be Tomorrow
I Just Can't Live This Way
Grave Of Doom – Grave Of Doom
Go Haunt Someone Else's Mind
With Your Doom Of Death And Grave

273. Here Comes Hell

The-Walls – Are-Dripping-Blood
My-Minds on Fire
Hell is Coming for Me
My-Soul is Burnt-Toast

I-Lived for The-Moment
Playing-With-Fire
I-Didn't-Give a Damn
Now-I'm – Paying-For-It

(Chorus)
Here Comes Hell
It's So Hellish Hot
Here Comes Hell
I'm So Afraid
Here Comes Hell
To Take My Soul Away

Partying and Lusting
My-Specialty in Life
I-Soaked-Myself in Evil
Enjoying – The-Evil-Laced
Ladies – That-Wanted to Party

Graveyards in Darkness
Ladies in Black-Dresses
Wanting to Be – Turned-On
By the Man – That-Knows-How to
Party – Very-Evil and Wild

(Chorus)
Here Comes Hell
It's So Hellish Hot
Here Comes Hell
I'm So Afraid
Here Comes Hell
To Take My Soul Away

274. Hell's Metal Monster

Burning-Down – The Road
Going-666-Hell-Miles an Hour
In-My-Metal – Soul-Burning-Machine
If-Your on My-List – Your-Soul-Will-Burn

Hired by Satan – He's so Rich
He-Has a Hobby of Buying-Souls
Souls-That-Need to Be-Collected
This is How-I – Make-My-Living

(Chorus)
Satan Wanted To Buy My Soul
I Told Him To Kiss My Ass
Satan Laughed And Handed Me Some Gold
I Laughed As Satan Marked My Soul A Little Bit
So I'd Be Evil Enough – To Drive Hell's Metal Monster

Touch of Evil – Makes-Me-Bleed
Angels-Better-Stay – Out of My-Way
Look-Towards-Your-Heaven – If-I'm-Too
Much – For-Your-Heavenly – Eyes to Intake

God-Does-Not – Seem to Mind
God-Has-Never – Stopped-Me-Once
Seems-Like the Damned – Don't-Mean a Damn
When it Comes to God's – Heavenly-Light

(Chorus)
Satan Wanted To Buy My Soul
I Told Him To Kiss My Ass
Satan Laughed And Handed Me Some Gold
I Laughed As Satan Marked My Soul A Little Bit
So I'd Be Evil Enough – To Drive Hell's Metal Monster

Take it From-Me – Sale-Your-Soul
Your-Name-Gets-Put on The-Bottom of My-List
Don't-Care – No-I-Don't – Greed is My-Heaven
When-Your-Name-Comes-Up – I'll-Run-You-Over
Set-Your-Damned – Soul on Fire – Like a Speed-Demon

(Repeat Chorus)

275. Death-Angels (Wings Of Steel)

Demons-From-Hell – Beware
Hell is Your-Domain – Stay-There
God's-Earth is Under – Our-Protection
Stalk or Hide – Will-Seek-You-Out

With-Wings of Steel – We-Fly
With-Swords of Light – We-Strike
Slicing and Ripping – Through-Your
Hell-Fire-Made – Demonic-Bodies of Filth

(Chorus)
Death-Angels – We Are God's Army
With Wings Of Steel – With Swords Of Light
We Fly – Searching For Satan's Demons
Earth Is Our Domain – Demons Beware
Demon's Blood – Wipes Off So Easy
Even Easier To Make It Flow Out
Of Demons Bodies So Bloody Fine

Humanity – Heed-This-Warning
Evil is Saturated – Deep-Inside the Earth
God-Gave-It to You – For-You-Not to Want-It
Heaven is The-Only – Forever-Answer

Speaking to Satan – Is a Sin and a Weakness
Turning-You-Towards – Favoring-Evil
Very-Soon – You-Will Become a
Demon on Earth – On-This-Day
You-Become a Target – That-Needs
To be Cast-Out – From-Earth
Straight to Hell – Paying-For-Your-Sins

(Chorus)
Death-Angels – We Are God's Army
With Wings Of Steel – With Swords Of Light
We Fly – Searching For Satan's Demons
Earth Is Our Domain – Demons Beware
Demon's Blood – Wipes Off So Easy
Even Easier To Make It Flow Out
Of Demons Bodies So Bloody Fine

276. When The Aliens Attack

Giant-Space-Ships – Spinning-In-The Sky
People – Freaking-Out-Everywhere
The-Man – Tells-Us to Relax
That-They – Got-It-Covered

At-The-Same-Time
They're-Pissing – Their-Pants

Every-Time-You – See-The-Man
They're – Sitting-Down-Sweating
Trying to Smile – That-Same-Old
I-Lie to You – Because-I-Can – B.S.

(Chorus)
Look At All The People
Too Scared To Scream
Looking Up At The Sky
Knowing They're Going To Die
When The Aliens Attack

The-Man-Tries to Talk to The-Aliens
We-Watch-Laughing – Under-Our-Breaths
Hoping-The-Aliens – Do-Not-Attack
We're-Happy – That-The-Man-Knows
What it Feels-Like to Be a Puppet

Waiting-For-Your – Puppet-Master to
Give-You a Tug on Your-Strings
When-They-Decide – You-Deserve-It

In-Horror – We-Watch as
Thousand of Smaller – Space-Ships
Come-Flying-Out of The-Belly of
The-Giant – Metallic-Glowing-Beasts

(Chorus)
Look At All The People
Too Scared To Scream
Looking Up At The Sky
Knowing They're Going To Die
When The Aliens Attack

277. Get Off That Damn Space Alien

Came-Home-Late – Space-Ship
Parked in My-Driveway
Not-Again – She-Promised-Me
It-Was-Over – Between-Them – My-Wife
The-Damn – Space-Alien-Lover – so
I-Kick in The-Door and Say to Her

(First Chorus)
What's Wrong With You
Get Off That Damn Space Alien
I Have Human Love For You
All He's Got Is Spaced Out
Alien Sex For You To Hate

I'm-Watching – Their-Non-Stopping
Not-Giving-Me a Care at All
It's so Damn – Weird and Nasty
That-It's-Starting to Make-Me-Sick
My-Wife – The-Damn – Space-Alien-Lover
I've-Had-Enough so I-Say to Her-Again

(First Chorus)
What's Wrong With You
Get Off That Damn Space Alien
I Have Human Love For You
All He's Got Is Spaced Out
Alien Sex For You To Hate

My-Wife – The-Damn – Space-Alien-Lover
Tells-Me to Shut-Up and Enjoy
I-Watch and Now-I-Know – I-Never
Wanna-Touch – My-Wife-Again
Hell-With-It – He-Can-Have-Her
So-I-Say to The-Damn – Space-Alien

(Second Chorus)
You Space Alien Prick
You Make Me Sick
You Ruined My Wife
Now She's A Filthy Hag
I Hope You Fly Off Together – And
Your Space Ship Gets Hit By A Meteor

(Evil Magic Wizard Wants A Son Trilogy: 278-280)

278. Young Lust Turns To Dead Love

(Story Teller)
Lovers in The-Tower – Making-Love
Spiders on The-Walls – Snakes on The-Floor
Their-Sharing of Love is Tainted by Evil-Magic
Soft and Tender – Turns to Climax
Young-Male-Lover – Loses-His-Breath
Dies-Without-Saying a Word – Young-Lady in Love
Screams-For-God to Help – Bring-Him-Back

(Chorus) (Story Teller)
Young Lust Turns To Dead Love
Evil Magic Wizard
Wants A First Born Son To Own
There's No Way Out
Father's Dead – Mother's Pregnant
Tied Up In The Tower
Her Life Ends – After Giving Birth

(Mother To Be)
Please-God – Help-Me
Please-My-Baby – Save-His-Soul
Save-Him-From – The-Wizard's-Evilness
Let-Him be The-Light – Not-The-Darkness
Please-God-Stop-This – Do-You-Want-This

(A Mother's Prayer)
My-Soul for My-Son's-Soul
Make-His – Mortal-Body
Useless to This-Evil-Wizard
Please-My-Soul for My-Son's-Soul

(Chorus) (Story Teller)
Young Lust Turns To Dead Love
Evil Magic Wizard
Wants A First Born Son To Own
There's No Way Out
Father's Dead – Mother's Pregnant
Tied Up In The Tower
Her Life Ends – After Giving Birth

(Evil Magic Wizard)
Pray-All-You-Want – My-Lovely
Your-Son – Will be Mine
You-Will-Die – Never-Knowing-Him

I-Promise-You-This – My-Son
Will-Drink and Bathe
In-The-Blood of The-Good

(Mother To Be)
Untie-Me – Set-Me-Free
Before-You-Make a Mistake
So-Grand – That it Will-Destroy-You
You-Are-Evil – You-Will-Lose
Good-Will-Always – Triumph in The-End

(Chorus) (Story Teller)
Young Lust Turns To Dead Love
Evil Magic Wizard
Wants A First Born Son To Own
There's No Way Out
Father's Dead – Mother's Pregnant
Tied Up In The Tower
Her Life Ends – After Giving Birth

(Evil Magic Wizard)
Stupid-Woman – You-Know-Nothing
Like a Whore – You-Laid-Down-Dirty
Out of Wedlock – With-Your-Lover
That-I-Killed – With-My-Dark-Magic

You-Will-Have-It so Much-Worse
I'll-Feed-My-Son – Your-Dying-Blood
Now-Drink-This-Gone – My-Lovely
Time-For-You to Sleep – Until-You-Give-Birth

(Chorus) (Story Teller)
Young Lust Turns To Dead Love
Evil Magic Wizard
Wants A First Born Son To Own
There's No Way Out
Father's Dead – Mother's Pregnant
Tied Up In The Tower
Her Life Ends – After Giving Birth
67

279. What Is A Evil Wizard To Do

(Evil Magic Wizard)
Wake-Up – My-Lovely
Time to Birth – My-Son
I-Waited – Long-Enough
That's-It – Look-Into-My-Eyes
See-Your-Short – Future-End

(Mother)
I-Prayed – This-Was a Bad-Dream
Evil-Wizard – You-Are-Foul so Evil
You-Will-Not – Have-Your-Day
Smite-You – Remember-This
From-My-Grave – I-Will-Laugh at You
I-Wish-I-Could – Look-In-Your-Eyes
When-You-See – Your-Triumph-Slayed

(Chorus) (Story Teller)
Evil Wizard – Evil Daughter
What Is A Evil Wizard To Do
She Is Not A Son – Her Mind Is Different
She Will Not Like Snakes Or Spiders
She Will Like Dating With Boys
How Many Boys – Will This Evil Wizard Kill

(Evil Magic Wizard)
You-Are-Weak – You-Are-Nothing
Your-Words-Strike – No-Fear in My-Soul
Mother of My-Son – I-Like-You
I'll-Let-You-Live if You'll be My-Wife
You-Must-Always be Loyal
While-Maidens – I'll-Enjoy
Say-Your-Answer – My-Lovely

(Mother)
I-Do-Not – Have to Die
You-Evil-Bastard – My-Mate-You-Killed
Just-For-Blood – You-Would-Kill-I
My-Shape is Large – Now-You-Want-Me
Your-Are-Sick – You-Are-Twisted
Burn in Hell – You-Evil-Bastard

(Repeat Chorus)
68

(Mother)
The-Thought of You and I – Makes-Me-Glad
I'll-Die-Without – Being-Defiled by Your-Touch
I-Hate-You! / I-Hate-You! / I-Hate-You!
God-Give-Me-Strength – The-Power of Your-Will
Let-What-Comes to Be – Kill-This-Evil-Wizard
Pain-My-Lord – The-Pain – My-Child is Evil!
Why is She-Not – Made-From-Light

(Evil Magic Wizard)
She! – No-This-Can-Not-Be
She! – You-Lying-Whore
What-Have-You-Done
God-Can-Not – Care for One-Like-You
Your-Lies – Will-Bare – No-Fruit

Dead-Already – Let's-See-My-Son
No! No! No! – This-Can-Not-Be
I-Have – Been-Cursed
I-Have a Daughter to Make-Evil

(Chorus) (Story Teller)
Evil Wizard – Evil Daughter
What Is A Evil Wizard To Do
She Is Not A Son – Her Mind Is Different
She Will Not Like Snakes Or Spiders
She Will Like Dating With Boys
How Many Boys – Will This Evil Wizard Kill

(Story Teller)
Down-Down – The-Spirits of The
Evil-Magic-Wizard – Fall-Downward
Into-The-Pit of His-Dark – Fearful-Heart

No-Son – Instead a Daughter in His-Hands
Her-Small-Face – Cracks-His-Foundation
When-She-Gets-Older
She-Will – Rip-Out-His-Heart

She-Weighs but Seven-Pounds
A-Ton is What – She-Feels-Like in
The-Hands of The-Evil-Wizard

69

(Evil Magic Wizard)
Dark-One in Hell – Where-Did-I go Wrong
Please-With-Evil – Change-Her-Into a Son

(Chorus) (Story Teller)
Evil Wizard – Evil Daughter
What Is A Evil Wizard To Do
She Is Not A Son – Her Mind Is Different
She Will Not Like Snakes Or Spiders
She Will Like Dating With Boys
How Many Boys – Will This Evil Wizard Kill

280. Growing Up Evil (In Three Parts)
I. Nice And Evil At Thirteen
II. Dating With Evil Inside Her
III. Lady Evil Is All Alone

I. Nice And Evil At Thirteen

(Daughter)
I-Love-This-Forest – Father
Everything-Is so Beautiful
Nature-Talks to Me – Like a Friend
I-Feel at Peace – Still-I-Ask
Why do You – Have to Be-Evil – Father

(Evil Magic Wizard)
Stop-Your-Prattle – It's in My-Mind
Making-Me-Feel – Good-Inside
I – We – Can-Not-Have-That – Can-We

(Daughter)
No-Never – I-Hate-This
Evil-Evil-Evil – That's-All-I-Hear
Every – Single – Day
Father-I-Want to Pick-Some-Flowers
Not-Butcher – Some-Animals

(Evil Magic Wizard)
Stop-That-Good – Thinking-You're-Doing
It-Will-Only – Make-You-Want it More
Daughter – You-Are-Evil to Your-Soul

70

Accept-It and Relish-All
The-Evil – Inside-Yourself
Daughter-This is My-Command
No-More – Pretty and Good
Dark-Lord in Hell
Is-Our-Master – Our-Souls-Are-His

(Chorus) (Story Teller)
Nice And Evil At Thirteen
Is No Way For A Young Lady To Be
Nice And Evil At Thirteen
Makes It So Hard On Her Soul
Nice And Evil At Thirteen
Prevents Her From Loving The Sun

(Daughter)
Father – Why-Did-You – Sell-Your-Soul
How-Could-You – You're a Fool
Why-Could-You-Not Leave
My-Parents in Peace and Alive

(Evil Magic Wizard)
Your-Father – Was a Weak-Coward
Your-Mother a Common-Whore
Daughter – I-Did-You a Big-Favor

(Daughter)
Father-I-Told-You – Not to Say-That
My-Parents-Were-Beautiful – You-Are-Ugly
Father-You-Give-Me – Nothing but Evil
I-Hate-Evil – I-Hate-You

Father-You-Want to See and Feel-My-Evil
Take-This-Stone to Your-Evil-Head
Bleed-More-Father – It-Looks so Pretty
Running-Down – Your-Evil-Face

(Evil Magic Wizard)
That's-It-My-Daughter
Now-Try to Kill-Me – Very-Hard
Very-Bloody – You-Are-Evil – Hate-Me
With-All-The-Evil – In-Your-Heart
If-You-Do-Not – You-Are-Useless to Me

71

(Chorus) (Story Teller)
Nice And Evil At Thirteen
Is No Way For A Young Lady To Be
Nice And Evil At Thirteen
Makes It So Hard On Her Soul
Nice And Evil At Thirteen
Prevents Her From Loving The Sun

(Daughter)
Father-You-Win – How-About-This
I-Kill-One-Animal – All-Bloody and Cruel
Then-You-Let-Me – Pick-Some-Flowers

(Evil Magic Wizard)
Flowers-Nothing but Flowers – Daughter
What-Did-I-Tell-You – About-Flowers
Daughter-You-Are – Scarring-My-Evil-Soul
With-All-This-Nuisance – About-Flowers
Alright-My-Daughter – Kill-Ten-Animals
Then-You-Can-Go-Pick – Your-Pretty-Flowers

(Daughter)
Ten! No-No-No – I'll-Get
Blood-All-Over – My-Clothes
Father-Do-You – Want-Me to
Hit-You – With a Bigger-Stone
I-Will-Kill – Five-Animals – No-More
You-Hear-Me – Father!

(Evil Magic Wizard)
Yes-My-Daughter
Go-Make-Your – Evil-Father-Happy
Turn-Your-Yellow-Dress
Blood-Red – From-Death

(Chorus) (Story Teller)
Nice And Evil At Thirteen
Is No Way For A Young Lady To Be
Nice And Evil At Thirteen
Makes It So Hard On Her Soul
Nice And Evil At Thirteen
Prevents Her From Loving The Sun

II. Dating With Evil Inside Her

(Daughter)
Father-My-Date is About to Come-Over
Father-Remember – Do-Not-Kill-Him
He's-Such a Nice-Date – I-Think-I-Love-Him
Father – I'm so Very-Happy – La,la,la,la,la

(Evil Magic Wizard)
I-Will-Chop-Him – Into-Pieces
If-He-Touches-You – Remember
This-My-Daughter – Very-Well

(Daughter)
He's-Here – Goodbye – Wait
Give-Me-Money – For-Beer and Weed
You-Know-How – I-Like-My-Dates to Drink
That-Way-More-Action – Less-Talking

Father-Relax-Your – Heart-Attack
I'm-Being-Evil – Like-You-Want-Me to Be
Ha,ha,ha,ha,ha – Goodbye-Evil-Wizard
Don't-Wait-Up – If-He's-Good-Enough
I-Might-Let-Him-Live – For-Another-Date

(Chorus) (Story Teller)
Dating With Evil Inside Her
At Eighteen Is A Pain
Good Date After Good Date
Say They Will Be So Good
That They Will Rock Her World
Then Nine Out Of Ten Dates
They Disappoint This Evil Princess
Then It's Off With Their Heads
For Wasting Her Evil Time
On Their No Good – Love Making

(Daughter)
Father-I'm-Home – My-Date is Dead
I-Can't-Get – His-Blood-Off – My-Dress
Father-Did-You-Hear-Me – I-Need a New-Dress!

(Repeat Chorus)

73

III. Lady Evil Is All Alone

(Evil Magic Wizard)
Daughter – Please – Daughter
I am Your-Father – Don't-Kill-Me
Remember-All-That – I-Did-For-You

(Daughter)
Shut-Up-Father – You're-Making-Me-Sick
Father-What-You-Gave-Me – Was a Life
Filled-With-Nothing but Twisted-Evilness
I-Don't-Need-You-Anymore – You're-Useless

(Chorus #1) (Story Teller)
Lady Evil Is All Alone
She Tried Her Best To Be Good
Lady Evil Is All Alone
Her Father's Blood Is On Her Hands
This Makes Her So Very Happy

(Evil Magic Wizard)
Daughter-Together – We-Are to Rule-The-World
That is Our – Dark-Lord's-Command

(Daughter)
The-Dark-Lord – Can-Kiss-My-Sweet-Evil-Ass
I'll-Deal-With-Him-Later – You-Die-First

(Chorus #2) (Story Teller)
Lady Evil Is All Alone
She Hates The World – It's Filled Up
With Too Many Good People
Lady Evil Is All Alone
Watch Out World – Here She Comes

(Story Teller)
So-Our-Story-Ends – In-Bloodshed
The-Evil-Magic-Wizard is Dead
Evil-Liz – Is-Evil to The-Bone
Just-Like-Her – Dark-Lord
Wanted-Her to Be – From the Beginning
Where in The-Name Of Heaven – Is-God

(Repeat Chorus #1 & #2)
74

(Bonus Song)

What Is Evil (Sweat In Hell) (568.)

You-Say – I'm-Evil
With-My-Words of Peace
Is-That-My-Fault – Mankind is
My-Friend – I-Love-Your-Souls
They-Taste and Burn so Great

Sometimes – They-Upset-My-Tummy
Giving-Me – Hellacious-Gas
Live and Let-Live – Mankind
Go-Ahead and Destroy-Your
Beautiful-Blue – Mother-Earth
I-Don't-Give a Hellish-Damn

(Chorus)
What is Evil – I Am
But Don't Worry About It
I Don't Even – Sweat In Hell
It's My Own – Fiery Paradise

Hell is Very-Vast – It's-Not
Half-Full-Yet – Rubbing-My-Hands
While-Licking – My-Lips
I-Can't-Wait – I'm so Hungry
Fools-Believe in Everything
If it's Spoken as Truth – I-Say to You-World
Hello – I'm-Not-Real – I'm-Only

The-Hate – Fear and Lust – Greed and Death
That-Dwells-Inside-You – Love-Can
Be-The-Answer for Salvation – Luckily
You-Believe in Me and My-Evil
To-Ever-Change – Your-Minds and Forget
All-About – Heaven and Hell

(Chorus)
What is Evil – I Am
But Don't Worry About It
I Don't Even – Sweat In Hell
It's My Own – Fiery Paradise

(Bonus Song)

Vampire Kiss (I Drink, You Lust) (552.)

Been-Around a Long-Time
Drank-Rivers of Flowing-Blood
Drank-Dry-Many-Human – Blood-Bags
I-Know-I'm – Blessed to Damnation
No-Angels – I-Ever-See
Is-God – Even on This-Earth
I-Don't-Know – It-Matters-Not

Time-Changes – Even-The-Undead of The-Night
Use to Be-Greedy and Thirsty
Until-I-Curbed – My-Blood-Intake
Then for The-First-Time – I-Got
My-First – Vampire-Hood-Wood
Which-Made-Me-Say

(Chorus)
Vampire Kiss – Living Lady
I-Drink – You-Lust
I Taste Your Scent
I Drink Your Blood
As You Purr And Moan To Ecstasy
Begging Me To Never Stop

I-Love-My-Living – Blood-Filled-Ladies
Throughout the Years – They-Change – I-Don't
They-Are-Such-Tasty – Female-Blood-Stock
I-Never-Drink-Down – Anything-But-Them

Another-Lady – Almost-Out of Blood
I-Stop-Drinking – Another-Dead-Lady – In-My-Arms
I-Drop-Her to The-Ground – Letting the Ghouls-Have-Her
She-Was-Fine – I'm-Thirsty-For-More-Blood

(Chorus)
Vampire Kiss – Living Lady
I-Drink – You-Lust
I Taste Your Scent
I Drink Your Blood
As You Purr And Moan To Ecstasy
Begging Me To Never Stop
76

(Bonus Song)

Vampire Kiss Baby (I Drink, You Suck) (Demo)

Been-Around a Long-Time
Drank-Rivers of Flowing-Blood
I-Know – I'm-Blessed to Damnation
I-Like-The-Ladies – They-Have-The-Best
Tasting-Blood – Flowing-Through-Their-Veins
Over-The-Years – They-Change – I-Don't

(Chorus)
Vampire Kiss Baby
I-Drink – You-Suck
Vampire Kiss Baby
You Taste My Vampire-Hood
When I Drink You Dry
Vampire Kiss Baby
You're Going To Love It To Death

I-Know – I-Taste-Great – You-Fine
Living-Lady – Blood-Stock
As-I-Drink-Deeply – From-Your-Thigh
You're-Almost – Out of Blood
I'll-Let-You – Finish-Me-First
Before-I-Take – My-Last-Drink

Another-Dead – Useless-Body
Laying-Dead – Beside-Me
I-Stand-Up – Pull-Up-My-Pants
Let the Ghouls – Have-Her-Now
I'm-Thirsty – For-More-Blood

(Chorus)
Vampire Kiss Baby
I-Drink – You-Suck
Vampire Kiss Baby
You Taste My Vampire-Hood
When I Drink You Dry
Vampire Kiss Baby
You're Going To Love It To Death

Hell Night At Demon House (Pages 78-98)

(Early Afternoon of October 31st)

(Ring,Ring) "Hello Mary, couldn't wait 'til I called you? Want me that bad, don't you Mary?"

"I'm not Mary, Kayden, I'm her friend, you know the hotter looking one, the one you want to get to know better."

"I do?" "Don't you??" "Just messing with you Lizzy. Yes I want you, I got the time. I want your body a few times before it's Mary's turn in a few hours. Then I have to rest up before all of us go to Demon House tonight."

"You're a dirty bastard Kayden. I don't know why I'm doing this, you kinda make me sick. I'd like to slap your face forty times."

"I'm sure you would Lizzy, maybe even forty one times. I'll tell you what you change your slaps to licks and you'll do just fine."

"I don't know, Mary's my friend. I love her like a sister, but I just got to know for myself the reason Mary smiles so big when she mentions your name, Kayden. My wonderful sexy, so manly built, ruler of Hell."

"Lizzy you don't have to talk your way into my bed you're invited, I'll gladly lust you for a couple of hours. I got to tell you Lizzy, before you would have never stood a chance in my Hell, to get your chance at a power up sex date with me. Damn Lizzy, you were so damn ugly before you had your all over surgery, you went from no way in Hell to Hell yeah, let's do it again, just give me a moment to rest first."

"That's the most romantic thing I've ever heard, you asshole. I'll tell you what Kayden, why don't you just F**k yourself for two hours, I'll even let you use my foot, you pretty face bastard, goodbye."

"Now, now Lizzy, don't be like that, I just want you to feel good about the new and much improved you. This is all new to you, you've never been hot before, it's a lot different for an unsuspecting lady like you to experience for the first time. Before, the man would have had to consume very large amounts of alcohol to the point of almost passing out before he said yes to you. Lizzy now you get to experience the other side of sex, where you are the one that is wanted and by the looks of you, you have enough to make a man weak and wanting more,

78

making you feel that power of control, that will change you into a power hungry vixen."

"You make it sound so great Kayden."

"It's not a great thing Lizzy it's a beautiful thing, especially since I get to be the one, the one that makes you start your metamorphosis to stardom where tales will be told about you and your hotness. And all you got to do Lizzy is hang up your phone and bring your fine ass over, for me to enjoy, 'til I've had my fun and am ready for a nap."

Fifteen minutes later / Ding dong / Come in / Kiss, kiss / Sex, sex, Give me a minute / Sex,sex / You were so great baby / Snoring.

Lizzy looks into the mirror, she can't believe how she looks, she looks so flushed and so beautiful. Lizzy's body is trembling from the way Kayden made her feel, his pillow talk, his large experience, he's all man and damn does he know it. Kayden told her not yet, to hold on and damn he was right, he was in total control. Lizzy looks deeper into the mirror, knowing what she wants, she wants Kayden to teach her to hone that power for herself, so she can be the one that owns the power. All men after Kayden will be her slaves that beg to have her body, her body that is so fine, perhaps the finest in all of Hell, she is ready to start making Hell talk about her like she is the Queen of it. Suffer boys and wait your turn. Hee, hee.

Lizzy brushes her hair, looking into the Mirror, loving the way she looks – When! The mirror begins to steam up, then starts to shake, scaring Lizzy and making her scream. It is a howling curse coming towards Lizzy with madness and rage for her blood. The mirror is shaking with such force it is about to fly off the wall. Silence. The mirror stops shaking then it shatters into many pieces, out comes.....

Bloody Mary, yelling, "You slut! You slut! How could you do this to me Lizzy? I am your friend, I'm the one that talked you into changing your appearance. You slut! I'm going to kick your ass. There's no way I'm going to let you try to take my place as Kayden's third lady of Hell. And by the way Lizzy, you still have a fat ass."

Lizzy yells, "You bitch, my ass is not fat. You're just jealous because you have a flat ass. And it is obvious the only reason Kayden would let a skank like you in his bed is because you are so nasty in bed and you have so much experience, you have become the queen slut of Hell."

Kayden is awake and enjoying watching two ladies fight over his pecker. (Pardon me, over him I meant to say) He thinks about saying something when, claws and fur begin to explode in an all out Hell Ladies cat fight. Mary runs towards Lizzy, hits her with such force that both ladies fall to the floor. They roll around on the floor tearing at each other like two crazy demon ladies, when they hear Kayden say to them. "Hey ladies look what I have for the both of you to enjoy together." They stop fighting long enough to look over at Kayden with his (?) at full attention. They get back up, kiss each other, then join Kayden together on his bed for some special kind of loving.

(Late Afternoon of October 31st)
(Snoring) (Giggle, giggle) Mary and Lizzy leave a naked, sleeping and very tired Kayden behind to have some girl fun. Mary is going to show Lizzy all about what it is like being a fine lady demon in Hell. Kayden's world is going so great but in one moment, Kayden will discover that even the ruler of Hell sometimes has some explaining to do. In walks a soon to be a very pissed off lady named Kelly, (Former Hell Witch of Purgatory, now Kayden's number one Lady of Hell). "What the HELL!!! Kayden you sorry Bastard, wake the hell up. On my BED!!! On my bed with your sluts. How dare you? Get your ass off my bed right now, you wash those filthy sheets, you sex pig you."

"Now wait a minute Kelly, I'm the ruler of Hell you don't speak to me this way."

"Shut Up! You Sex Pig! I mean this little to you? Kayden how could you do this to me? I know you are with your dirty sluts when you are away from me, but on my bed."

"Our bed you mean." "Shut Up! Don't you correct me, I'll, I'll bite your Hell snake right off you if you piss me off anymore than I am right now."

"Baby I'm sorry, things just happened and I lost track of the time. What time is it anyway?"

"Who gives a **** what time it is? What? You have to go do it again? Huh you sex pig?"

"Stop calling me sex pig, because baby, that ain't cool."

"That ain't cool? Well how about this?"

Kelly takes her right foot and kicks Kayden right where he does not want to be kicked, making him fall to the floor instantly from the immense pain of it. "See what you get, sex pig? Now on your feet and out the door, naked you go, oh mighty ruler of Hell."

"Come on baby let me back in, I need to take a shower."

You should have thought about that first before you were with your sluts on my Bed!"

"Baby at least give me some clothes to wear. Baby? Baby I have to go to Demon House tonight."

"Well go naked, stinking of sluts you sex pig."

"Damn it, alright I'll go but you make sure you show up tonight for your part at Demon House. You hear me Woman?!"

"Yeah I hear you, and you can eat my shit. You hear me Man?!"

"Yeah I hear you Kelly, now tell me you love me."

"I hate you." Kelly replies. Then she says "*****************".

Kayden turns around to walk away from the shut and locked door he is staring at and spots some Demons looking at him and laughing. "Demons you think this is funny? I'll show you funny!" Kayden explodes into madness and takes it out on the laughing Demons. They try to run away but Kayden is so full of rage that he even goes after innocent Demons whose only crime was that they were walking by at the wrong moment in Hell. One hour later Kayden is calm, covered in Demon's blood and staring at hundreds of dead Demons that have been torn apart. Kayden says, "**** it," and leaves to go clean himself up.

(Early Evening of October 31ˢᵗ)
Kayden is leaving the apartment of his secretary Alice. He went knocking on her door after Kelly kicked his ass out of their house. Alice is his second lady of Hell and a big hater of Kelly. Alice opened her door to Kayden with a smile, she cleaned him up, fed him then made love to him. Kayden feels better and thinks about going back to his house to make sure Kelly will show up tonight at Demon House. He decides against it and gives Mr. Dark a call telling him to go to his house to make sure Kelly knows that she has to show up. After hanging up he looks up at a public clock on a wall, he still has some

time left, so he heads to Styx Bar & Grill for some food, Beers and some Hell weed.

I walk into Styx Bar & Grill, look around and see a lot of the same faces that are here every time I want to feel better. These faces are lucky I'm in a better mood, they can thank Alice for this. What is going on in my mind, is that there seems to be a lot of demons that do nothing but drink and get high in Hell. I wonder what their jobs are? Skip it I'll worry about that another time, for just like them I want to drink and get high. As I am heading towards the bar, I hear her, Becky and her loud personality. There's something that I emit that makes the Demons of Hell know when I'm getting ready to be close to them. Just like every time I open a door, Demons look at me and try to make themselves seem like they belong in Hell and at the same time they bow their heads in submission to me. 1-2-3- (On cue) Becky yells out, "Kayden, I'm right here, just give me second and you can buy me a drink."

Sometimes I answer her, sometimes I don't, like right now, I just keep on walking, passing by Demons who wish I would drink and smoke somewhere else. Like clock work, I'm standing at the bar and Becky is standing right beside me, looking and smelling so good, wearing something tight that shows off her big beautiful twins. I look at Becky, she is impatiently waiting for me to give the bartender my order for she knows that silence is what I want until I get my order out. I stop talking, Becky starts talking and probably won't stop talking until I leave. I'm staring at Becky's chest as she tells me her great news, she's getting married. I feel like being an ass, so I say to Becky, "What about me? You know I don't share my women, so you cannot get married." Becky looks at me with unbelieving eyes, she cannot believe the words I said to her, I smile and tell her that I'm just messing with her.

"Oh Kayden, thank you so much. My heart almost stopped, I love being yours, whenever you want me but I'm in love and best of all I found someone that loves me for me and not just for my body," Becky says.

I'm getting ready to congratulate Becky as my beer and weed show up. I open my mouth but Becky is still talking, I wait for over five minutes for her to stop talking. I nod my head barely listening, looking at her, wondering to myself if I should **** her one more time for the **** of it when there is finally silence.

"Congratulations Becky. I am happy for you. You are a beautiful woman, whoever this Demon is, he is lucky to have you."

"Thank you Kayden. I'm so happy that you are happy for me."

"Well Becky let me meet this lucky Demon." Becky smiles, gives me a great big hug and calls for her Man to come over to meet me. What a D-bag this fool is. He comes over to me all attitude. I ignore it at first because I know what is going on in his feeble mind. That Becky was mine first and with the snap of my fingers she would be again just like that. I congratulate them both again and try to walk away. Becky stops me with a great big goodbye hug. Then Mr. Idiot the Demon runs his mouth one too many times and I have no choice but to beat him down like the fool he is in front of his woman and everybody else at Styx Bar & Grill. I tell the fool and Becky to go away but just like most fools they don't know when to stop. Then he comes back at me wanting to spill my blood. A moment later he is just a dead blood spot that I am walking over to find a table to sit down at, so I can relax before I head to Earth. Becky walks up to my table crying, she looks at me and says.

"Kayden I'm so sorry. Kayden please forgive me. Please don't take out on me what the man I thought I loved said to you."

"Don't worry Becky, we're cool. I did not want to do that but he left me no choice."

"I understand completely Kayden, let me make it up to you." Becky falls to her knees in front of me, grabs my right hand and sexually tries to lick her dead loves blood off of it.

"Becky stop this you don't have to do this and I don't want you to. Just take a seat and have a drink. It will do you some good." Instead of getting up Becky is trying to undo my pants, when I pull her hands away. "Stop it Becky," I say loudly. She finally does.

We sit together in silence, drinking and smoking when she says, "What a dumb ass he was. Do you want to **** Kayden?" So we take off our clothes and let the drinkers and smokers of Styx Bar & Grill watch us like we are all alone. When we are done I tell Becky to take a vacation and not to give up on finding love.

(In Hell – The Evening of October 31st)
Kayden, Mr. Dark, Bloody Mary, Lizzy Borden and a Demon named
Bruce are walking together to the Gates of Hell, to exit Hell. Bruce
was a man that died and went to Heaven, but when he got there he
pissed off God, so God stripped him of his halo and kicked his ass to
Hell. Kayden met Bruce at Styx Bar & Grill, Bruce was just about to
get the Hell kicked out of him for F***ing four Very big Demons'
women. Kayden stopped the blood slaughter, killed the four very angry
Demons, then he and Bruce drank, smoked and enjoyed the women of
the four, now dead, Demons the rest of the night. They became friends,
Bruce is a lot of fun but is still in the habit of getting his ass in trouble.
So Kayden is making Bruce come with him to Earth as a penance
because Kayden had to kill some more of his Demons, six this time.
Which left six lonely women that Kayden had to please because to
Kayden that is the least he can do for them, for making them all
widows.

(On Earth – The Evening of October 31st)
Thirteen friends are making their way to Demon House to party and get
laid. There is suppose to be a fourteenth friend coming to the party as
well to make them the safe number seven as couples but unknown to
these thirteen party goers the fourteenth person is really Kelly,
Kayden's number one and very pissed off lady of Hell. Kelly set this
party up at Demon House by going back in time to Earth to the year
1988, and seducing a limp fool into believing that Kelly liked him.
With him wrapped around her finger with the promise of sex, this fool
did what Kelly told him to do by inviting only twelve of his friends so
all together they would be the perfect number thirteen, which is just
want Kayden needs. Halloween is the day. Thirteen is the number.
When their souls expire on this day, instead of their souls going to
Heaven or Hell they are forfeited to the ruler of Hell, which is Kayden
of course. It is a one time a year big time power up that Kayden will
receive if everything goes as planned.

(Hell) Bruce is in the rear, watching Mary's and Lizzy's asses, telling
them both how fine their asses look to him. They giggle then tell him
to keep on looking and suffer from wanting them. Bruce laughs loudly,
real funny and demonic, saying "Ass grabbing run B-yyy". Bruce, the
fastest human Demon in Hell when he's sober, speeds up to Mary and
Lizzy and grabs both of their asses, picking them both up into the air
from the mighty force of his quick hard squeezing. Mary and Lizzy are
dropped back down to the ground, mad as Hell, swinging at nothing, as
Bruce is in front of them about twenty feet smiling and touching
himself.

"Stop that you Freak," Mr. Dark yells out to Bruce.

Bruce looks at Mr. Dark and says, "Why? You want to touch me instead?" Mr. Dark gets mad and goes after Bruce, wanting to tear him apart. Bruce laughs and runs up to Mr. Dark and slaps him across the face a few times then runs away, leaving Mr. Dark so mad that he would agree to anything if he could get his hands on Bruce. Bruce absorbed at the moment in having some fun at Mr. Dark's expense does not pay attention to Mary and Lizzy, who are still pissed as Hell, coming up behind him to beat him down. Mary and Lizzy are the perfect tag team, they hit Bruce high and low knocking him down to the ground. A second later, Mary and Lizzy are stomping the Hell out of Bruce, yelling all kinds of nasty, nasty things to Bruce for being such a (Your Nasty Word Here), then Mr. Dark joins in on the stomping of Bruce.

Kayden is just about to say enough of this shit, when out of nowhere Demon Eyes comes up from behind him with Kayden's own spiked bat (which Demon Eyes stole) and sinks it deep into his back making Kayden roar out pain and anger. With a quick pull the spiked bat is freed and smacked across his face, making his face look like mush. Kayden looks at Demon Eyes as his face and back begin to heal. She is so sexy in her leather outfit, long blond hair streaming behind her and wearing a mask to hide the face that Kayden wants to see.

"Kayden Hart, the Devil of Hell, one day soon you will die by my hands. So says Satan, who you slayed, making me his assassin after his death. You had no right, you are just a lackey of God and you will pay for your crime and your sin against my dead master Satan. So says I, the finest human Demon lady in Hell, Demon Eyes. I am a feast for your eyes, while I dig out your insides. Need I say more?"

"Hello crazy lady, I've missed you, why don't you take off your clothes and come over here and sit on me," Kayden replies sexily.

"In your dreams false Devil of Hell, I am too pure for your wicked lust."

"Prove it." "What?" "Prove it." "How?"

"Take of your clothes let me know for sure if you have been touched by a man or if you're as pure as you claim to be."

"Yeah right – perv."

"I knew it, you're a slut."

Demon Eyes looks at Kayden like he just ripped out her heart and stepped on it. "You know Kayden you are a real bastard, you don't know who I am."

"Yes I do." "No, you don't." "Yes I do."

"Even if that is true you still would not know the real me."

"What the Hell are you talking about?"

"I'm talking about respect, you horny bastard, respect for being the person that I am and not one of your Hell sluts that you lust like there is no tomorrow. No Kayden I am not your toy, you will never have me, you remember this as I take my leave of you."

"You know Demon Eyes, I still don't think that it has dawned on you that you have a pattern. First you attack me, all full of rage then you stop. Second you give me your spiel about how you are going to kill me. Third, well that is my pattern, I try to turn you on. Fourth you get mad and offended and walk away just to do this over and over again. You're kinda bent, you need some help and you do not want to kill me, you want me to set you free."

"Never will I want that! But since you believe this, which makes me sick inside, I'm going to hit you where it will hurt you the most."

"Take your shot!"

"You don't want my shot as you say. It won't be at you but at the one who you lust the most in the Hell you rule, your precious Kelly. I will rip out her eyes and chop her into pieces with your very own spiked bat."

" You stay away from her!"

"Oh I hit a nerve, she's one dead bitch you bastard, hee, hee."

"Demon Eyes, I like you. You're my kinda of crazy for a great crazy time but if you touch my number one, I will turn from horny devil of

Hell to something, I don't want for you but I will make come to life if you push me too far."

"I'm so scared, look at these," Demon Eyes spreads open the top of her leather outfit reveling her beautiful breasts, then puts them away and runs away laughing, shaking her fine ass.

The four that are accompanying Kayden, stopped what they were doing when Kayden roared out, they watched not knowing what to do. Mr. Dark and Bruce have encountered Demon Eyes before but Mary and Lizzy have no idea who she is and why she wants to kill Kayden.

"Kayden?" "Yes Mr. Dark."

"Let me take care of Demon Eyes for you she is getting out of control."

"No, Mr. Dark I'll handle her in my own time."

Bruce says, "At least let me chase her down so you will know where she is hiding."

"No, Bruce it's okay I already know where she is hiding."

"And you know who she is?"

"Yes I do Bruce." "Who is she?"

"That is a secret Bruce, one that I don't know the outcome of. Let's get the Hell out of Hell and have some fun destroying thirteen party goers minds before we kill them and take away their souls for me to feast on like a big o' trick or treat bag full of candy," Kayden commands.

Mary and Lizzy walk up to Kayden and get real close to him trying to comfort their ruler of Hell. "No time ladies, maybe tomorrow but I don't know for sure, for I have some mending to do with Kelly about our little three way afternoon delight we had together."

"Well if she is stupid, give me a call," Mary says.

"Yeah right if Kelly is stupid then Kayden will be calling me not you." Lizzy says to Mary. Before anything can escalate, Kayden says enough and the five of them continue their way to Demon House.

(The Legend of Demon House)

Demon House is wherever it needs to be every Halloween. It was created by Satan for a once a year power up of thirteen souls that he gets to gobble up making him stronger year after year. The first time like many times after that Satan infected a house that was having a Halloween party, he showed up as one of the party guests, mingled with the crowd of many and picked out thirteen of the purest souls that he wanted to devour. As the night went on Satan started with one, then two working his way up to thirteen. Satan wanted all the souls at every Halloween party but thirteen is his limit, by God's command. Satan a very smart ruler of Hell never took any chances, he always made sure that there was plenty more than thirteen at every party. Satan has batted a thousand since the inaugural one. Kayden a different ruler of Hell for the fact that Kayden was once human and Satan the very famous first fallen Angel from Heaven. Kayden has been to many of these Halloween parties himself and is batting a thousand as well, so with big balls Kayden is doing something that has never been done before, including by Satan. Thirteen souls only at tonight's party, one shot, no mistakes just the way Kayden wants it to be, to show a watching God that he better take heed, for Kayden will prove one day that he is something that God should have never created.

The Six that are playing the Demons this Halloween night and their power that will make this night a living breathing Hell for thirteen humans that want to party and get laid.

Kayden: The Devil of Hell – An Unlimited Powerhouse, including the power to make the walls bleed and the power to pull a soul out of a dead human with only one mighty pull.

Kelly: A Demon that use to be the flesh eating Hell Witch of Purgatory, with her Demon claws she can rip the flesh off of any party guest before their blood stops flowing and gets cold.

Mr. Dark: A sneaky Demon that will mess with the minds of the party guests, making them believe that he is a good Demon that wants to help them out alive.

Mary: A Demon who can use any reflection as a portal to come through and cause a lot of bloody carnage.

Lizzy: A Demon that uses any object that has a blade or a pointed end as a portal to come through and cause even more bloody carnage.

Bruce: A fast Demon that will run through the house causing drafts and scary sounds, that will make the party guests run around scared.

(Side-note of Hell) In Heaven and Hell, time has no meaning, but in Purgatory and on Earth time is a constant. One hundred years in Purgatory is one thousand years on Earth. As told in the book Purgatory's Full there are two outcomes for Earth (and it's up to you to believe whichever outcome you want to believe happened). The first story is that a small but big enough asteroid hit Earth and caused almost all of mankind to die off, then God snapped his fingers and made life start over again, causing mankind to live underground for almost two thousand years while the Earth healed. When they came out to the light they were different, evil had been erased and all who died got to go to Heaven. The second story is that mankind had themselves a big horrible World War III and now on Earth only half of it can support life. Whichever story is the truth, happened a little bit after Kayden Hart died in the 2050.

(Another Side-note of Hell) Even though in Hell time has no meaning Hell keeps constant track of the time that is passing on Earth, down to the second. Even though this Halloween night ritual can only happen every one Earth year it does not mean that, that year has to be the one, Satan used, and now Kayden has to use. There is a magical object in Hell that is called the "Blood Stone" it allows the user to go back in time to whenever they want this Halloween Hell night at Demon House to happen, even if that time already had its Demon House. The power that fuels the "Blood Stone" is a single drop of blood from God himself. Satan one day crawled himself out of Hell all the way to Heaven, when he got there with one of his talons he reached out and scratched God making him bleed. Satan then ran back to Hell, protecting the single drop of God's blood on his talon. When Satan got back to Hell he placed God's drop of blood inside a black stone, when it became sealed, the stone turned from black to blood red. Satan knew he had a big power in his hands but was surprised when this stone gave him the power to travel back in time on Earth, instead of a big power force against God that he was expecting to have from it.

(Kelly in Hell) "Tomorrow is another day, but today Kayden my sweet love and sex pig, you are going to pay for what you did to me. I know you love me in your own way and I the same. Hell is a such an easier life than Purgatory was. I don't know what's the matter with me? Really, how do I think that I can get away with telling Kayden the ruler of Hell how to get off? Then again who the hell does he think he is?"

"I am his woman, his #1, I don't know why he even wants his sluts? I am better than Ten of them, for I am an Eleven, that Kayden cannot do without. I have you ruler of Hell right where I want you, but I know you, out of nowhere you know already and are ready for what is getting ready to happen, well about 80 percent of the time. No Kayden you are not perfect and you think you can take on God? God's going to kick your ass and you even know this, but your damn wings, you have to have them, they're your white whale, your garden of Eden."

"Why can't you be satisfied with what you have? You are the ruler of Hell and you don't even enjoy it to its fullness. Would you be happier if you lost your rule and became just another damned soul that will be tortured, probably by me? Like I said Kayden, my sweet, my sex pig, tomorrow is another day and today is today, the day you pay the price for thinking that you can treat me like this. Even if you're the ruler of Hell, you use to be human Kayden, which Satan never was and sometimes I wonder if he treated his #1 more humane than you do? I love you Kayden but I cannot let you keep breaking my heart. I deserve better than this for all the Hell I had to go through just to get to Hell, to be just right where I am now, not taking your shit anymore, you lovable, pretty faced, sex pig, that I love with all my heart. Why can't you love me with all your heart Kayden? If you did we would rule Hell together, making everybody but a few of our friends as miserable as Hell can be. I would love that, but no, you have to be so damn selfish, don't you Kayden?"

(Earth) The Year is 1988, the location, an old abandoned spooky house in the thick south with a local legend. It has been lit up by generators, tables have been set up with snacks, punch and liquor. Six ladies and seven guys are ready to have some Halloween fun including a seance, that will bring out the Demons to feast on the souls of the unsuspecting thirteen party guests.

(Hell) The five to Earth travelers, pause at the Gates of Hell, which is made up of dried Hell's fire, bones and flesh of the damned. "Good evening Mr. Hart."

"Good evening , Larry and Peter. Has Kelly come back through Hell yet?"

"No sir. Not yet, sir. She missed her daily afternoon appointments," Larry replies.

"She probably just felt like staying home to rest up for tonight's feast of mine."

"Yes Sir," they both say in unison.

"Okay then go ahead and open up the gates and if Kelly has not shown up in an hour, so I can come back here and take her back through time, then give her a call and tell her that I demand her to show up here immediately."

"Yes Sir," they both say in unison again and open up the Gates of Hell.

"Larry and Peter, whoever calls her better be in the best of voice for she is pissed at me and might just reach through the phone and rip out your tongue, for pissing her off even more."

(Pause) "Yes Sir," they both say in unison, scared for their lives.

(Still in Hell) The Gates of Hell open up to Kelly standing there on the other side waiting, like she is in the spot that she is suppose to be and the other five are late as usual. She is dressed to party, looking so hot that Kayden wants her on sight. Kelly loves this very much.

Kelly – "Well just don't stand there looking at me, wishing and wanting, get you asses on this side so we can get this over with."

Kayden – "Hey Kelly you look so fine, come over here and give your Ruler of Hell a kiss."

Kelly – "How about this Kayden, instead of giving you a kiss, how about I give you a kick to the front of your pants?"

Kayden – "Still pissed at me I see. Well no matter you look fine and after I devour thirteen souls, you and I are going to have some long fun with our clothes off."

Kelly – "Sex Pig!"

Mary – "What did you call my Ruler of Hell, you ungrateful witch?"

Lizzy – "Yeah Witch, maybe you should be burned at the stake."

Kelly – "Shut up you sluts or I'll kick both of your asses!!!"

Mary & Lizzy – "Bring it on Witch bitch, flesh eating hag."

Kelly – "That's it sluts. Bloody Mary huh, I'll make you bleed slut and Lizzy you slut, you are still a skank inside and you will always be."

Kayden – "Enough of this you three Hell cats, let's get to work."

Kelly so fast and dangerous, strikes Mary and Lizzy with all claws out ripping their faces into bloody messes. They try to get away from her, only to have Kelly use her flesh ripping claws on their backs, arms wherever she can strike and make bleed. Kayden looks over at Mr. Dark and Bruce, watching the both of the them back away from the cat fight they are watching, not wanting any part of it including trying to stop it. Kayden laughs and steps in the way of Kelly's claws, stopping her from doing any more damage to Mary and Lizzy, only to take the full rage of their shredding. After about a minute of ripping Kayden into bloody pieces, Kelly finally stops, steps back and admires the blood she made flow.

Kayden – "You through Kelly or do you need to vent some more?"

Kelly – "I haven't decided yet. Do any of you want me to make you bleed some more? (Silence) That's what I thought. Mary, Lizzy you sluts just give me a reason and I will finish shredding you."

Kayden, already healing, walks over to a crying and shaking Mary and Lizzy, grabs both of them by their arms, and with the power of the Ruler of Hell inside him he speeds up their healing with his mighty force. With all six of them ready to go, Kayden grabs the Blood Stone that he's wearing around his neck as a necklace and opens the portal that leads them back in time on Earth to the year of 1988.

(Earth) Six couples drink, smoke and get turned on as the lonely thirteenth wheel drinks, smokes and wants to get turned on. Everybody is not worrying about the seance at this time and want to separate to find a place so they can be alone and have sex in a scary ass house on Halloween night. The boombox is blasting out "South of Heaven" by Slayer when the door opens hard and fast making the boombox stop playing instantly out of fear. All thirteen Halloween party guests stop what they are doing and stare at the open door as Kelly walks in so sexy, lovely and evil looking.

92

Adam the Fool is so happy, Kelly is so out of his class, the other six men would drop their dates in a Hell's moment to switch places with Adam the Fool. Kelly loves this, by taking in the moment that she is the most beautiful human, Demon Lady of Hell. Kelly walks in looking at the six ladies that wish they were her and that hate her so much for being so much more beautiful than them. The only sounds in Demon House you can hear are heartbeats and the footsteps of Kelly walking into the room like she owns it.

Sexy Kelly, commands Adam the Fool to walk over to her. When Adam the Fool is almost in arms' reach, Kelly commands for him to stop walking. Adam the Fool waits in ecstasy for his next command by his beautiful mistress of the dark. Kelly, showing her long teeth, snaps at Adam the Fool to get on his knees, he drops so fast that the fall to his knees hurts him and makes him grunt out. Kelly laughs out loud so evilly, telling Adam the Fool how pathetic he is, Kelly then sticks out her right foot and tells Adam the Fool to lick her shoe. Adam the Fool shaking with nervous excitement, puckers his lips and gets ready to do what he is commanded to do. His lips are almost upon Kelly's shoe when she says "Trick or Treat", after a moment of silence, laughter fills the air as thirteen Halloween party guests, calm their fear and excitement. Kelly acting like a human now helps Adam the Fool off the floor, when he is on his feet, she gives him a great big hug, making his back crack. With no kiss following for Adam the Fool, Kelly takes over the party, making the weak thirteen humans do exactly as she says. Thirteen Halloween party guests, drink and smoke themselves into total Fucked-up-ness, while Kelly thinks about Kayden with hate.

Kelly looks around, she has taken her time, it is almost 12 o'clock, two hours later than Kayden wanted the seance to happen. She laughs out loud, thinking about how Kayden's face looks right now, all mad that she has not done what she was told to do. The clock strikes twelve and Kelly says to thirteen people that are F**ked up that it is time for the seance. (The seance is not very important in the scheme of things, it's just a big over dramatized way for Kayden and the others to make their entrance to the party.) Kelly still in charge says some scary ancient words, making the seance as scary as she can, then all of a sudden she stops speaking and after a pause she says two more words, "Sex pig", and laughs out loud then says, "Come on then Kayden get your thirteen souls if you can, you sex pig you."

Kayden and the others hear this, Kayden says, "What the F**k is she doing?"

Kayden looks at four faces that can't believe what is going on, shakes his head, talking out loud to himself, "How much shit do I have to put up with before this is over with?" Kayden commands all pissed off, for the others to follow him, when they reach the door to Demon House, Kayden with madness kicks the door open knocking it off its hinges. Thirteen Halloween party guests scream as five Demons enter their Halloween party, looking to spill their blood and rip their souls out of them.

Kayden to Kelly, "Well thanks a lot Kelly for F**king every thing up for me."

Kelly smiles unafraid and says, "You're so very welcome my darling. Did you happen to wash your sluts off my sheets you damn sex pig!!!?"

Kayden looks at Kelly, Kelly does not flinch one bit. "I have had enough of you today Kelly, I am the ruler of Hell and the best looking thing to ever enter Hell, get over your pettiness, come over here right now and tell me that you are sorry for what you have done."

"What I have done?" Kelly responds back so madly that her screaming makes the glass in almost every window shatter to pieces.

Kayden now wanting to be an ass to Kelly says all smart ass like, "Yes what you have done, you dumb witch." Kayden with a smile on his face looks at Kelly and her expression, makes his smile fade away very fast. Kelly blinks with madness flowing through her like she has never felt before in her life or after her death. "Calm down Kelly and don't go all crazy forgetting who I am," Kayden says to a shaking with madness Kelly.

Kelly stops shaking and then gives Kayden a great big smile, Kayden feels relief, then like a speeding, pissed off, very hurt Demon Lady of Hell, Kelly rushes toward Kayden, grabs a hold of him and throws him so hard that she makes him go flying through the wall all the way to the outside of Demon House. Four Demons are staring at Kelly, she looks over at them and says, "Boo." Kelly goes so fast after Mary and Lizzy and restarts the shredding that they both deserve so very bad.

Out of nowhere Mr. Dark says to Kelly, "Kelly stop this madness right now I command you."

Kelly stops what she is doing, looks over at Mr. Dark and says, "Shut up you limp, nothing happening, speck of nothing or I'll come over there and rip off your face and stick it up your ass."

Mr. Dark thinks about saying something but walks away with his head down in shame, which makes Bruce the Demon start to laugh his dead ass off. Kelly looks at Bruce and says, "Stop laughing or I'll stick your wuss head right up Mr. Dark's ass, so far you'll never be able to pull it out again." Kelly is just about to re-start ripping Mary and Lizzy to shreds, when there is this loud, demonic roar out of nowhere, scaring her frozen.

Kayden rushes back into Demon House so pissed off that he forgets all about his plan and goes right after the thirteen Halloween party guests like a blood and soul thirsty, Ruler of Hell. In mere moments Kayden has ripped out twelve humans souls and ate them all up like they were candy, he pauses looking for his thirteenth morsel, who's hiding behind Kelly like a frightened child. Kayden walks over to Adam the Fool and right before he can eat his soul, Kelly reaches out and rips the Blood Stone right off Kayden's neck. Kelly grabs a hold of Adam the Fool says the magic words and just like that they are gone to somewhere else in time.

Kayden stares at the nothingness and then roars out so loud that Demon House crumbles to pieces right on top of him and the rest of his comrades. After a few moments Kayden and the rest are out from under the rubble, with no way to get back to Hell. Mary and Lizzy beg Kayden to heal them so they can stop bleeding all over the place and for their faces to stop looking like Hell stomped on them.

Kayden shakes his head and yells out loud F**k many times, kicking the rubble around him, away from him like an angry spoiled child. Mary and Lizzy keep begging Kayden until he finally stops kicking everything in sight and finally heals them, so they both will shut the Hell up and he can think of a way to get all of them off Earth and back to Hell where they belong. Four human Demons look at Kayden with fear of the coming sun that will melt their flesh right off their bodies, so very painfully until there is nothing left of them to melt, which is the only way they can get back to Hell without the Blood Stone.

Right before dawn, with about fifteen minutes to spare, Kelly shows back up and demands that Kayden apologize to her for what he has done.

Kayden replies back to Kelly very madly "My ass I will," and then demands that Kelly give back his Blood Stone that instant.

Kelly with no Fear of Kayden says, "Tick- tock asshole, apologize or burn!"

"Then I'll burn you witch."

"Fine see you in Hell, and just to piss you off even more," Kelly stops and smiles then quickly grabs a hold of Mr. Dark, Bruce, Mary and Lizzy says the magic words and poof once again they're gone, this time leaving Kayden all alone on Earth covered in blood watching the sun rise that will melt his flesh, blood and bones to dust.

"Well God I guess I have to endure some more pain, this time as an apology to Kelly for being an ass. What can I say God? I'm the Devil of Hell, being bad and evil is in my nature. And honestly I like it, being the Devil keeps me hard as the day is long. Well thanks God for the chat, guess you don't feel like pulling my fat out of the fire and sending me back home to Hell. That's okay I understand, you want me to feel this pain for being cocky. I made history God, this is the first time that thirteen souls have not been devoured by the Devil of Hell on Halloween. So since I did not get all thirteen, here you go God, take your twelve souls that I forfeit to you, due to my failure." With his claws, Kayden rips opens his chest, exposing his dark heart, freeing the twelve souls, that were now nesting so nicely inside his Devil's body, then Kayden painfully burns them to burning ash.

(In Hell the Morning of November 1ˢᵗ) Kayden, kicks himself through the Gates of Hell, stomps himself through Hell, causing trouble, making Demons run away from him, for their lives. Then Kayden turns back around and makes his way back to the Gates of Hell, causing more havoc on his way back. Kayden exits Hell and heads to his home, which is located outside of Hell. Kayden stands in front of his door, pissed as the Hell he rules, he opens the unlocked door, walks in and there stands Kelly. What will Kayden do?

"Kelly?" "Yes Kayden?" "Love you"

"I love you Kayden. Do you think it worked Kayden? Do you believe God bought it?"

"Yes I do, for his silence spoke clearer to me more than any words that he would have spoken."

"Is it time Kayden?"

"Almost."

"What do you mean by almost Kayden?"

"Kelly all I have to do now is wait 'til God, who thinks I'm losing control of my Hell, to play his trump card."

"What is his trump card Kayden?"

"Angel Eyes." "Angel Eyes? How will you deal with her Kayden?"

"That is so simple Kelly, I'm going to sic Demon Eyes on her."

"Do you think that you will be able to trust her? To control her?"

"Yes I do."

"How can you be so sure that you will be able to do this?"

"That is also so simple Kelly, I'm going to sic you on her."

"Me?" "Yes you."

"How can I defeat a crazy lady like that Kayden?"

"That, Kelly, my fine lady, is a secret to be told to you right before your battle with her. Now come to me my love so I can take you in my arms and carry you to our bed."

Hell Night At Demon House (The Song) (235.)

Halloween – Party-Night
At-The-Old – House of Horrors
Stories of Blood – Staining-The-Floors
From-The-Demons – That-Live in The-Walls

Play-With-Death – Life of The-Party
I'm-Very-Lucky – Tonight – an
Angel-Demon From-Hell – Is-My-Date
Kelly – She-Can-Have – My-Soul
As-Long as I – Feel-Her-Fire-First

(Chorus)
Happy Halloween – It's
Hell Night At Demon House
My Blood Will Flow Like Wine
When Demon Kelly From Hell
Takes My Soul Before Daylight

I'm-Adam-The-Fool – The-Last of Thirteen
Alive – I-Don't-Want to Die – Tonight
I-Want to Live – Forever
Kelly is Protecting – My-Life
From-The-Devil – Named-Kayden-Hart

Kelly-My-Savior – Grabs-My-Soul to Save
Back-In-Time – We-Fall-Together
My-Life is Saved – But-No-Taste
From-The-Sexiest – Demoness-From-Hell

(Chorus)
Happy Halloween – It's
Hell Night At Demon House
My Blood Will Flow Like Wine
When Demon Kelly From Hell
Takes My Soul Before Daylight

(Repeat Chorus)

Something Extra (943.) (Bonus)

What is That – It's so Small
Watch-Out – It's-Moving
It's-Alive – While it Looks-Dead
A-Hole is Opened-Up in Its-Center
Is-That – Black-Blood – Now-It's
Turning-Red – Yes – It's-Blood

I-Was – Feeling-Good
Now – I-Don't-Know
Almost-Like – My-Soul-Is
Being-Penetrated by Evil
I'd-Like to Frown – But
All-I-Can-Do is Smile

(Chorus)
There's Something Extra
Inside My Soul
It Is Evil – It Is From Hell
Where Is God – I Don't Know
And I Don't Care

Can-You – Feel-This-Evil
Must be For-Only – Me
Damn – What a Day
I-Guess – I-Don't-Need
This-Six-Pack of Beer
Or – This-Sack of Weed

This-Evil is Calling to Me
If-I-Was-You – Right-Now
I-Would – Run-Away
For-Very-Soon – I-Will-Change
What is This – You-Ask
It's-Simply – The-Devil's-Heart

(Chorus)
There's Something Extra
Inside My Soul
It Is Evil – It Is From Hell
Where Is God – I Don't Know
And I Don't Care – Anymore

99

(Bonus 7 Inch) (Pages 100-101)
Dead Souls Hate The Living (731.)
(Side – **A**) / (Written: 04-07-2015)
Grave Breath (735.)
(Side – **B**) / (Written: 04-08-2015)

Dead Souls Hate The Living (731.)

Dead-Souls – Hate-The-Living
The-Spider – Eats-The-Fly
What is In-Your-Closet
Will it Rip-Out – Your-Soul
If-You-Dare to Open it Up

Wider-Wider – Open it Up
Nothing is All – You-See
Blink-Your-Eyes – Look-Sideways
Something is There in The-Waiting
Silent by Fear – Vision so Clear
You're-Going to Die – Bloodily

(Chorus)
Rip – Rip – Rip
Dead Souls Hate The Living
They Rip Into Your Flesh
To Get To Your Soul
So Shiny It Comes Out
Then Turns To Rot In Their Hands
As They Absorb The Life Out Of It
Rip – Rip – Rip
Dead Souls – Hate The Living

Dead-Souls – Hate-The-Living
All-The-Warmth – All-The-Life
Believers of Fear and Doom
Are-Their – Midnight-Snack
Those – That-Have-Belief
Are-Their – Main-Course
Pray-All-You-Want – Just-Don't-Look

(Repeat Chorus)

100

Grave Breath (735.)

Worms in Your-Eyes
Maggots in Your-Stomach
You-Are-Dead and Rotting

Lady's-Still in Love – With-You
Wants-You-Back to Life
Resurrection is Your-Future

Chicken's-Blood – Eye-Of a Killer
Your-Hair – And a Rose-Petal
Boiling so Nice – In a Pot

(Chorus)
You Have Come Back To Life
You Have Grave Breath
You Have Come Back To Life
You Are So Very Hungry
You Have Come Back To Life
You Are Going To Eat Her Face First

One-Lady – Eaten-Up-All-Raw
Your-Dead-Soul is Still-Hungry
You-Smell – Meat in The-Air

Alive-Flesh and Blood-Bags
You-Scream-Out – Agony-From-The-Grave
Lick-Your-Lips – Chomping on Meat

(Chorus)
You Have Come Back To Life
You Have Grave Breath
You Have Come Back To Life
You Are So Very Hungry
You Have Come Back To Life
You Are Going To Eat Her Face First

Bullet to Your-Brain – You-Are-Dead-Again
Back to Your-Grave – You-Go to Stay – Having
Grave-Breath – Only-You – Can-Smell-Forever

(Repeat Chorus)

101

The Invention Of My Mind Rockin'

I've always been a fan of music, classic rock, rock and roll, hard rock and heavy metal. I've also always been a fan of movies, comedy drama, action, suspense, fantasy and horror. As a kid my hobby was writing lyrics that I created in my mind. In 2013 I took my hobby, my passion for music and movies and with them I created Mind Rockin'. By doing so I made myself become something that I never thought or dreamed of doing before and that was to become a self-published author. My creation of Mind Rockin' works like this. I sit down in front of my computer and come up with a melody or score in my mind to go along with the original songs or lyrical stories that I am creating. However when you the reader/singer reads or sings the song or lyrical story, there is no right or wrong for the melody or score that you come up with in your minds, be it rock and roll, pop, country or rap. Mind Rockin' is a concept I created for persons just like myself, those of us that would like to be able to do or create something like stories or songs but with no opportunity knocking at the door this dream of ours stays that, a dream. Mind Rockin' is the only thing in the world where the person you are has the chance to use what's inside you instead of the usual way where it is only one way for everybody, and that is the way the creator intended for it to be foretold or heard.

I'd like to dedicate this book and thank my Wife of Twenty-Four years, I love you Christina thank you for your Love and Support.

I'd like to thank all my Family and all my Friends. Thank you to all my Fans, I am a Fan of yours as well, together We can make a difference. Let's Shout It Out and Speak As One.

The Gemini Rising Rockin' Machine.

Discography: Books 1 Through 19

Book One: **Who Am I?** – 1-20

Book Two: **Mind Rockin'** – 21-40

Book Three: **Big Time Love** – 41-60

Book Four: **Love High** – 61-80

Book Five: **Siphon Your Minds** – 81-100

Book Six: **Do You Remember Rock And Roll** – 101-120

Book Seven: **Rock And Roll Bachelor** – 121-140

Book Eight: **The End** – 141-160

Book Nine: **Sunshine Dealer** – 161-180

Book Ten: **Thunder Love** – 181-200

Book Zero: **The 2.0 Versions Of Who Am I? & Mind Rockin'**
  (**13** New 2.0 Songs & **12** Gift Songs)

Book Eleven: **Dog Day Apple Pie** – 201-220

Book Twelve: **The Pig People Are Back** – 221-240

Book Thirteen: **Gemini Dance** – 241-260

Book Fourteen: **Gemini Beast** – 261-280

Book Fifteen: **Pink Hearts** – 281-300

Book Sixteen: **Sexual Amnesia** – 301-320

Book Seventeen: **Party In Your Panties** – 321-340

Book Eighteen: **Rock Or Bust** – 341-360

Book Nineteen: **Fucked Up** – 361-380

www.ingramcontent.com/pod-product-compliance
Lightning Source LLC
Chambersburg PA
CBHW070508130626
46555CB00003B/1207